JONATHAN COUZENS

TO BE A LION

FROM CUBS
TO KINGS

First Published 2024 by Jonathan Couzens

Copyright © 2024 Jonathan Couzens

www.honeybadgersafaris.co.za

ISBN 978-1-0672377-2-1 (Print)
ISBN 978-1-0672377-1-4 (Ebook)

Cover and interior crafted with love by the team at
www.myebook.online

FOREWORD

To write about animals is to make educated guesses. At the end of the book, I have included scientific references relating to some of the animal behaviour described in this story. Often findings and theories are refined later or may even contradict one another. It would be incredibly foolhardy to presume we know it all.

What is true of an animal in one area is not always true of an animal in another area, as they are designed to adapt to their environment.

This story is based on behaviour I have personally witnessed in the Kruger National Park while conducting safaris on behalf of Honey Badger Safaris. The deeper information is gleaned from scientific papers. The animal-human conflict is also based loosely on real events. I have endeavoured to maintain its accuracy with the knowledge we have now.

Although this is a work of fiction, I have included real places, existing lion prides like the Vurhamis, and male lion coalitions like the Gomodwanes, who currently rule the area around Crocodile Bridge in the Kruger. By the time you read this they might be long gone. The people written about are fictional and any resemblance to anyone alive or dead is coincidental.

Jonathan Couzens

CONTENTS

CHAPTER 1

At the base of Muntshe hill lies the Mlondozi dam, surrounded by grassland as far as the eye can see. This savannah is what many imagine Africa to be. Basalt soils support creatively named grasses – blue buffalo grass, finger grass and stinking grass. Marula and apple-leaf trees emerge like exclamation marks from the pasture, with none more iconic to the African scene than the flat-topped umbrella thorn tree.

This vast environment can fool you into thinking it is devoid of life. But if you take binoculars, trees become giraffe, boulders become elephants, shrubs become ostriches, and shadows mirage into wildebeest. A game of Where's Waldo brings forth wildlife. The granophyre soils of Muntshe hill rise above the basalt plains where they host toxic candelabra trees. Sunlight glints off weathered rocks. Purple-pod terminalia trees and large-fruited bushwillow trees shade some of these rocks on which plated lizards, rock monitor lizards, and sometimes black mamba snakes sunbathe.

You can hear the fish eagle call from his roost near the dam. The black, white and rusty-red bird of prey flies on the updraughts that rise off the hill into the often-blue sky punctuated with cumulus clouds that provide scale to the scene.

Mlondozi picnic spot sits next to Muntshe on a hillock, offering views over the dam, onto Muntshe hill, and the grasslands below. In the summer it's a gin and tonic view – green, with the dam full; khaki and coffee in the winter, with the dam low. To the east, the rhyolite hills of the Lebombo mountains rise like a rolling wave out of the savanna. We call them mountains, but you would laugh at that description if you were from Switzerland.

The scale of the big sky is intoxicating. Grey go-away birds call their rude namesake call of 'Go awaaayyyy' and a host of insects buzz in the heat of the day. The emerald-spotted wood dove gives its mournful call, the sad call at odds with the scenery. The dam is burgeoning. A herd of Cape buffalo wade at the edge of it, spilling into the grass with vocalisations like cattle punctuating the cicada's buzz. Little isolated disputes erupt between herd members but, overall, it is tranquil, the heat suppressing their energy. The buffalo in the water are indifferent to the crocodiles while some buffalo graze more safely on the plains. Hooves dig into the soil and plough the land. Others replenish the nutrients in the soil with their dung. Some are eating, ploughing and fertilising simultaneously. Several of the dark beasts stare into the distance. They are large and pitch-black. The bulls have a thick helmet-like growth at the base of their sweeping horns called a 'boss' which gives them a formidable look.

Their ears below the horns shoo the flies that swarm. Snow-white cattle egret birds follow the herd, riding some buffalo like Kelly Slater rides a wave. Buffalo can weigh up to eight hundred kilograms; this bulk moving through the grass disturbs tasty insect treats for the birds who glide down and predate the fleeing bugs. Some buffalo lie down with their hooves tucked under them, chewing the cud. The sweet scent of the herd floats on the gentle breeze.

A tower of giraffes becomes a journey of giraffes as they move towards the water. The gait of these tall animals appears slow, but because of their stride length, they rapidly cover distance. Red-billed oxpecker birds on the giraffe's necks eat ticks and parasites, moving up and down like construction workers. The buffalo herd hosts these birds along with the rarer yellow-billed oxpecker. Their hissing 'churr' call erupts with a dispute over a tasty tick.

The lead giraffe's long dark tongue comes out and moves busily around his nostrils as he walks. His head has two ossi-cone horns, rubbed bald from settling duels for females with his head. He is over five metres tall and takes a few steps at a time, then stops and scans the scene. He walks like a camel with both front and back legs moving simultaneously on the same side. Left side together, then right side together.

He feels an instinctive compulsion to be cautious when approaching waterholes. He is diligent, and he looks into the distance, up to the picnic spot and then scans down. His fellow herd members follow his lead. They are a tower again.

The buffalo stare at the giraffe. The giraffes goggle back at the associate ruminants. The fish eagle throws its head back and belts a far-carrying 'Weeeed- ahhh, hhyo, hhyo, hhyo.' The cicadas are silent during the call, and the bush is still after it ends. Gradually the cicadas pick up their buzzing again. Crested francolins make a shrill, repeated in and out cry, 'Kwwerri-ketch, Kwwerri kwwetchi.' On the far side of the dam, the giraffes and several buffalo gawk towards the sound. It does not repeat, and the giraffe stares and flicks his tail from side to side, the thick hairs on his tail cutting through air sounding like a brush through coarse hair.

A pathfinder buffalo cow chewing the cud stands up and stretches, her muscles shuddering. A hippopotamus breaks the dam's surface with a snort, spraying water into the air as a mist. He emits a loud sound like an obese laugh. A few moments later, another hippo further down the dam replies. The giraffe nears the water's edge, and his compatriots follow his lead. He halts a few metres from the edge and gazes. Movement in the water startles him, and the giraffe turns and steps away. He angles back towards the water and glares at the offender – a terrapin swimming under the surface. Egyptian geese paddle in the water and his leer turns to them.

Another buffalo gets up and stretches. A few more follow suit and one or two head towards the grasslands. The giraffe swings his attention to the buffalo and watches their movement as they plod towards the grass. A buffalo snaps his head back, scratches his flank with his horn, and repeats until the itch is gone. The action unsettles the giraffe. He rotates and moves towards those following him. He steps, halts, and turns, facing the buffalos. The buffalo vocals increase and the sounds of the buffalo's hooves grow louder. The young buffalo in the middle jostle with the marching orders. Growl-like sounds emit from the herd.

Then they move in single file into the tall grass. Cattle egrets take off from the ground and settle. A neon-blue and white woodlands kingfisher spreads his wings in an apple-leaf tree near the water. He opens his beak – red on top, black beneath – and calls 'chit -trrrrr.' Blacksmith lapwings start their call. The call sounds like a blacksmith hitting metal 'Klink, klink, klink.' The birds intend to dive-bomb buffalo to divert them from their nests on the ground. The buffalo are indifferent to this courage and plod on.

It is summer; dust does not rise, and the ground is damp. Rains have fallen in the past weeks and the pasture is lush for the buffalo. The giraffe ogle at the procession; some gaze in different directions, looking for any sign of movement, any sound or smell. Their instinct compels them to. The lapwings calm and halt their metallic call. The buffalo's path is not endangering their camouflaged ground nest. The giraffe treads towards the dam and peers into the water, scrutinising for movement. Content, he extends his front right leg sideways, then the left, repeating in increments until his front legs are spread wide. His head comes lower and lower towards the water as the legs open, his lips break the surface, and he drinks, frozen in this awkward stance as he pumps water into his stomach. Then, with a jump, he closes his legs. Water sprays from his mouth, and his head reappears in the sky. He gapes towards the buffalo and watches them move.

Fellow giraffes stand next to him, and synchronised drinking begins.

CHAPTER 2

F ive buffalo, their pelts crusted in mud, have not got up to join the herd. Older and all bulls, they can't move like they used to. The mud, water and foliage around Mlondozi spruit call and they no longer follow the herd. They stay near resources. One is missing the hair from most of his body, which gives the appearance of smooth rock, no longer ebony but a grey granite. White patches on his face through wear and tear, two worn patches where his ears rub when flicking away flies and horns gnarled and knotted like the bark of a dead leadwood tree. His eyes are dark brown like milk stout with blue horizontal oblong pupils floating in the middle, enclosed by wrinkly circular folds and eyelashes. His wide black nose is moist, with nostrils flared.

Bald buffalo can't see as well as he used to or move as he once could. Deep scars streak his flanks from encounters with his nemesis. He is wise to the wilderness life; he watches the herd, hears the calls and looks to the horizon. He glares back towards the giraffe, going up and down towards the water like synchronised cranes.

The breeding herd disperses but the buffalo bulls remain. Water drips from the giraffes' mouths as, saturated, they turn and begin to walk off. The first giraffe stops. The others halt and follow its gaze, staring towards the same point, tension in their body language. A kudu barks from Muntshe hill, unseen. A chacma baboon's bark echoes, continuous and monotonous. The kudu's bark joins with other baboons, the cicadas go silent.

A presence of power.

The buffalo rise. The giraffes are no longer stoic. Breaking into a rocking run, their front and back legs power together, propelling them forward. Amber eyes watch the fleeing giraffes with dark circular pupils. Movement attracts them, but giraffes are not on the menu today. Patiently waiting for the large herd to move off, they have a penchant for buffalo. They know they are close enough. Fanned out in position, escape is impossible, though the outcome of the battle is not a foregone conclusion.

They emerge into the open plains. Nine lionesses and eleven sub-adults. The lead lioness melts out of the grass onto the hard-packed mud full of spoor marks. The buffalo face outwards in a circle, their heads lowered, glaring at the lions with upturned noses. They snort and stare at the lions as tension fills the air. Some might query the title of a lead lioness, and indeed there is no alpha female in lions like in a hyena clan, female lions are egalitarian. But when this lioness walks, the pride follows, and so we call her the lead lioness, knowing that tailing her often allows for spectacular sightings.

The lionesses' focus is razor-sharp, heads erect, ears down, and measured steps, some in the habitual hunting crouch. The lead lioness leers, focusing on one buffalo, the oldest bald buffalo. The lion's instinct tells her this is the one. He snorts and gives a short rush; the lead lioness relinquishes ground. The blacksmith lapwings raise their metallic alarm call. The crested francolin shouts his. The combatants ignore them. Old buffalo spins and returns to his compatriots.

The lionesses stride closer, the buffalo lose their nerve and bolt. The lead lioness sprints, heavy grace on four paws. Muscles bunch and ripple like pythons working beneath her fur. Her compatriots dart in from all sides, following the bald buffalo like heat-seeking missiles, their heads steady despite frantic sprinting bodies, trailing tails snaking for balance. Two lionesses hit together with claws and paws, forearm muscles surging with the effort. A lioness springs to latch on, but slips, rolls aside, and is back up fluidly.

Another lioness leaps and alights the buffalo's back, claws slashing deep. The buffalo loses his footing and plummets, skidding along the dirt. The lead lioness tumbles off but is up on her paws in a flash, as both predators converge towards the neck. Two buffalo storm in with heads down to aid their confederate, horns pointed towards the attackers.

The lionesses disperse and scramble to safety. The old bull rises, standing dazed and urinates in his adrenaline-filled state. The urine streams from his penis, positioned where most expect his belly button to be. It snakes with the pressure of the stream. His buffalo partners rush, separating the lions in different directions.

The lead lioness creeps in again for the bald buffalo. This time he does not flee but faces her with horns, eyes and courage. She studies him, and he glares at her. He lunges, and she yields like a matador. Animals shout; the ground shakes with buffalo stampeding towards the tawny cats. Her eyes remain on bald buffalo. She looms and he charges again, she sidesteps, and his momentum carries him past her. The bull bellows, and his compatriots congregate beside him.

Nine lionesses stand watching, panting, and the buffalo gaze back. An impasse. The sub-adult lions have been observing but start to creep nearer. The lead lioness lies down like the sphinx. For a moment, it appears the lion and buffalo are indifferent to each other. The sub-adults inch closer and closer. The buffalo snorts and, with nifty pace for an old bull, he grunts and goes all out, rushing at the cats with animalistic might.

His life depends on it.

The youngsters skip away from him, some tag him on the rear, and as he spins, they retreat, keeping out of danger range. Hooves and paws churn up an earthy smell with the underlying scent of wild jasmine, as the buffalo crush the shrub, the pleasant smell discordant with the battle.

Impalas feeding in the thickets add their alarm snort to the scene. The sounds of alarm and desperation combine to make hair stand on end, and stomach knot. Even if you have never heard it, you're instinctively cognisant of danger. A primal fear.

The lead lioness studies the scene as the bald buffalo spins and twists, trying to protect himself. A young sub-adult lioness stalks the bald bull; she crouches down with her head low, her rear in the air, teasing the bull into action. The fit buffalo chase her, and she bounds away but returns and crouches in front of

9

the bald bull. The old buffalo charges. She retreats, and the bull stampedes through as the lions disperse. He circles near the other bulls, but a little distance has opened between the bald bull and his allies as his brother buffalo move further away each time, as they tire and instinctively move from danger. Bald bull becomes an island.

He ploughs, turns, and bucks as the young lions tease and cajole. One alights on his back briefly but slips off before she can get a grip on the spine. A young male sub-adult catches a glancing blow from the buffalo's hooves. He staggers at the impact but moves away without impediment. The tail of the buffalo circles with his movements, and the lions' tails flick for balance as they dance a dance of death. The lead lioness observes. Another lioness comes and lies by her, they watch the bull tire, calculating when to get involved.

His bellows, snorts and growls are frantic and desperate, and his movements stiffen. The sub-adult lions slip closer and closer without reaction. The lead lioness rises, strides, and vaults from her back legs. She seizes the bull with her paws on his rear, opens her mouth wide and bites down near his spine. Lionesses hit him from all sides and snatch onto his flesh, while he stands defiant. The cats hang off him like heavy coats on clothing hangers. One leg gives, and down he crumples; his comrades rush to his defence, and the lions sprint.

The bull vocalises his fear, and blood streams from a nose wound, but he revives and rises, although he is hurting. His compatriots stand beside him.

In a semi-circle, the lionesses face them. The sub-adult lions stand back, several with mouths open, panting with effort, others with tails flicking in agitation. A growl is emitted, the lead lioness steams in, the buffalo run. She targets the bald bull, and he can't keep up with his fresh brothers. Launching her body into the air, she lands near his rear, straddles him and bites into the flesh covering his spine.

He turns, and she slips off with the momentum. He stampedes towards her as she scrambles out of reach of his horns. Other lionesses try to mount his rear and the collective weight of the lions causes him to falter, and he crashes and rolls. Buffalo circle back and come in at speed with their horns, trying to hook a cat. The lionesses scatter in all directions emitting snarls.

The bald bull rises again, his stance defiant, his nose high, but the deep red blood streams from his nostrils. He lowers and sweeps his head up in a hooking movement. Blood flies into the African sky. The air fills with its metallic smell as the blood from his nose is joined by more blood from a wound near his anus. He urinates again, the stream splashing onto the ground, mingling with his blood.

His cronies are charging with vigour in his defence, as he stands alone, spent. Lions flee in every direction, a mass of claws and tawny muscles straining. The lead lioness watches the bald buffalo through the melee with her amber eyes and the island of a pupil they hold. The other buffalo move further away and stand in a row, four staring towards the bald bull, watching his efforts. He has been in this position before – he has been in *their* position before.

Bald Buffalo sighs and tries to buck with airborne hooves. He is unable to. He crab-walks in pain towards the lead lioness. She moves to the side and launches, her front legs and claws hug his broad neck as her mouth clamps down on his muzzle.

Dangling by her claws, with her rear legs slashing and raised so that her body is kept away from heavy hooves, the buffalo wears the lead lioness as a necklace. She keeps the pressure on, a hanging dead weight. Her breath mingles with the buffalo as he slows.

The other lions sense the end is near and swarm in. His buffalo brothers make to rally, but a lioness rushes at them, and they bolt away. He stands alone with twelve lions hanging on him. The lead lioness keeps her grip on his muzzle but moves her lower body away from what she knows must come. He crumples, the lions roll and pin him down. The lead lioness relinquishes the muzzle and grabs the throat, as another lioness clamps the buffalo's mouth and nose. One more lion joins the lead lioness throttling the bull's thick neck as the rest of the pride anchor the buffalo to the ground.

His legs kick the air, his brethren bellow from afar, his kicking becomes weaker and weaker until it halts. She holds the throat, feeling the pulse beneath her teeth. Warm salty blood trickles into her mouth, and she breathes through her nostrils as she squeezes. She only releases once the pulse is still.

Then she stands and pants over her prey, her entire body heaving with her panting. The lions lick the buffalo, emit growls, and their paws strike out as they jostle for position, gravitating to the easy entry point – the anus. The lions enlarge this opening through the thick buffalo hide. The lead lioness claims the cheek meat on the face. They gorge them-selves on as much meat as they can, pelts turning dark with blood. Eventually, with stretched bellies, they walk some metres away and laze in a food coma.

The lead lioness looks up as a bateleur eagle descends. A tawny eagle comes down, and white-backed vultures soon follow. The pride would drag the carcass to the shade and hide it from the vultures if it was closer to a tree, but now they just watch the vultures, especially the resident male lion coalition.

The sun slips under the horizon, the oranges and hues of the sunset lost on the lioness; she can't see the range of colours we can. However, once twilight descends, her eyes allow her to see better than us. The design of her eyes concentrates the starlight and moonlight, illuminating the nightscape. She pants with a belly full of buffalo, watching the night wash over. Comfortable as darkness envelopes. Not wanting to draw any attention, she holds back her inclination to roar.

The sub-adults are on the kill; some are inside the carcass, blood matting their fur, and several are in the ribcage. Putting her paw to her cheek, it comes back with blood, unsurprising as she has had her head in a buffalo. But it is tender – a gash on her left cheek from a horn slash. She rolls onto the other side and falls asleep.

CHAPTER 3

Later, the lioness wakes to scan her surroundings. She can hear them, the three dominant males, a roar in the distance but moving her way. She compels herself up and goes to relieve herself before staggering towards the carcass and eating. The other lionesses hear it too. The roars get closer and closer until they shake the ground. She eats as much as she can, and then over the carcass, a massive mane appears and teeth bare with a growl that reverberates and paws that slash out at any that dare to growl back at him. It materialises into a three-headed beast as his brothers-in-arms join and the lionesses and the sub-adults scatter.

The three males settle down to eat what remains of the buffalo. The lionesses walk away and lie down – the boys will eat themselves into a coma. The lionesses groom themselves and lick each other, the hooked papillae on their tongues working the blood from their fur, reaffirming their bonds and reconnecting after the disputes around the dinner table. A few scratches are groomed and pasted with saliva; the lead lioness receives lots of love due to her cheek wound. She lies content as another lioness grooms the wound that will scar her.

A thunderstorm starts in the distance, and they doze in and out of sleep during the night. Once or twice a hyena makes a furtive attempt, but a lion charge sends her on her way. Black-backed jackals try their luck, circling at a distance. The male lions wake them with a symphony of roars, with a 'this is mine, this is mine, this is mine' roar. Letting all know who the boss is, they roar their territorial announcement just before the dawn when the sound travels further, instinctive wisdom. The lionesses ignore the first round but can't help but join in on the second, all roaring as a collective, announcing their claim to the land. The Mlondozi pride and the Nkumbe male coalition rule these parts, telling all with ears.

The sun rises to find the three males bloated, on their backs, sleeping. The females are on the kill, eating, not with the same intensity but still giving it a good go. Many mouths make light work. By mid-morning, lions lie over the dam banks with paws in the air and full bellies. Some drag off little morsels which the circling hyena commandeers, as well as the black-backed jackals. Lions don't baulk at stinky meat and will eat carrion like we eat pizza.

The picnic spot is burgeoning with tourists, binoculars pointing as the news spreads. The gentleman who looks after the picnic spot watched the entire hunt unfold. Picnic spot visitors gawk at the tawny bloated objects in the sun. The lead lioness walks large-bellied to an ebony jackal-berry tree on the bottom of the Muntshe hill and the others follow. But after they leave the immediate vicinity, the hyenas move in for the carcass. The lead lioness whirls back growling, her face contorted in anger and the hyenas and black-backed jackals scatter in all directions. A chorus of laughter comes from the picnic spot.

The lead lioness tries to drag the carcass, but even though it is feasted on and lighter, she only moves it a few inches. She gives up and pants, and glares up at the vultures in the trees and then back to the hyenas. Another lioness joins her, and they haul the carcass towards the shade. Another lioness joins, and eventually six lionesses heave the carcass to the shade, hoping to eat the rest comfortably. But then a Nkumbe male charges and claims the carcass as his own. Swiping and growling, his brother comes, and they snarl for a second until each finds a different piece of carcass real estate. The third male joins after this commotion, and they feast.

The lionesses languish in the shade of the jackal-berry, waiting for another turn of the carcass. A crocodile has come out of the dam and heads to the stomach contents and offal left from the carcass. He smells the remains and gets a few intestines for his trouble as hooded vultures use their small beaks to pick up a few leftovers. The hyena, white-back vultures, and a lappet vulture investigate the titbits but wait for the main carcass.

The Nkumbe males eat and eat until they need to sleep again. One of them, a big lion, has a yellow-orange inner mane that encircles his broad face with a dark black mane encircling that. His mane is like steel wool in all directions, and the black hair continues along his belly until under his legs. His dark mane extends along his back on his spine to past the shoulder and front legs. His amber eyes have large round dark pupils – pupils that the rest of the world shrinks from when they look at you. The world becomes small indeed when he gazes upon you. He has white marks under his eyes that help reflect the starlight into his eyes.

The lips around his mouth are black, contrasting with his yellow teeth. His long canines are visible when he pants, his bottom jaw hangs slack, and his entire belly heaves as he tries to force air over his tongue to cool himself down. Long white whiskers sprout from around his mouth and the snow-white hair under his chin is now red with buffalo blood.

His tawny pelt wrinkles over his muscles. Large veins criss-cross his belly carrying his lifeblood to vital body parts. His paws are massive, and when his claws are retracted like now, the long hair and soft paws give him a benign comical look, which is deceiving. His face is covered with the scars that wild living and hunting bring. His two brothers have similar body sizes. One has the tip of his tail missing, and the other's mane is blond, not black.

The large black-maned lion moves towards a puddle made by a lioness. He places his muzzle in the urine, inhales, then lifts his face and grimaces. A flehmen grimace, he's forcing her scent into his vomeronasal organ. The organ is on the top of his palate, and as the scent reaches it, he downloads informa-tion. He moves his face from side to side as he buffers the information. This organ connects to his brain; he moves to another puddle and repeats the process. Black-mane is checking whether any females are in oestrus or season. He likes what he downloads and he moves over to the lionesses and smells their hindquarters. He gets one or two growls of discouragement but they're half-hearted protests. Black-mane squirts over the female's urine and scratches his back legs simultaneously, marking his ownership.

Half-tail, the short-tailed male lion, notices, stretches and yawns, then also goes to download information from the lioness's urine. Blondie continues to eat, his stomach burgeoning with protein. The three large male lions are content in their domain. Blondie pants heavily and stares at Half-tail, then leaving the meal he strolls towards his comrade and rubs his face against his brother. Then after doing the same with Black-mane, the three brothers collapse in a pile near each other.

CHAPTER 4

The young male lion that was kicked by the bald buffalo licks his wounds. It's his third rainy season and his mane is short. He's larger than his female siblings but his body hasn't filled out yet. He has three other male siblings that were born at the same time: one brother from his mother and two males from a lioness sister. The lionesses can synchronise their oestrus and nurse cubs that are not their own, providing a common creche for the pride that helps to raise the youngsters.

This particular young lion enjoys harassing leopard tortoises when he finds them, often on the tar road after rain, placing water in their bursa sacs from the water puddles on the tar. He picks them up and carries them as water gushes out from the bursa sac as a predator defence. Many a human has mistakenly thought a tortoise is urinating on them when handled. Leave it be, and you won't deprive it of its water supply.

The young lion ignores the liquid and gnaws on the shell. The lionesses observe, but they do not join in, though his siblings are sometimes involved. Once, he managed to break off some of the hard shell as he chewed but eventually he had to give up after hours of effort, and the tortoise plodded away with a badge of honour on his cover and copious amounts of lion slobber. Because of these observed proclivities, he's named Ufudu or tortoise in isiZulu. He's fortunate I'm not a research scientist, then his name could have been H21632, for some people say we should not name animals. He would then be just a lion, which he is, for most. But not for you, as you've made his acquaintance now.

His direct lion brother found a porcupine in one of the drainage pipes under the road, the culverts where they like to hide during the daylight hours. He got a few quills in the paw as the spikey animal backed into his clumsy efforts. The sounds of the quills rattling, and the hissing and snarling from the lion brought us to the sighting, like a hyena towards impala alarms. The porcupine survived, and so did the young male lion, thereafter with the moniker Jelwana, Tsonga for porcupine.

The third young male stumbled across a honey badger. The honey badger is renowned for its courage, humans have shared this knowledge but animals have to glean this for themselves in the wild. The sound of this encounter also drew us. With his thick loose pelt, the badger squirmed around in his skin and, to the young lion's horror, bit and raked him whilst still in the lion's mouth. The young lion opened his mouth, and the badger fell to the ground yet did not retreat but rushed at the young lion with his tail erect and spitting murder, infuriated at the young lion's presumptions. Despite his earlier intentions, the lion fled at full speed from the small creature with a courageous heart, a lesson in resilience and courage having been dished by the black and white animal.

We, therefore, named this lion Insele, which means honey badger in isiZulu.

The fourth male is the timid one. He hangs back and only joins in when the others have started and thus has no scratches, scars, or stories we have seen. So he is simply named Timid.

Recently there's been a subtle change in how these young lions are treated. Ufudu and his male siblings are not as included in the grooming. Their fathers are getting shorter tempered with the brothers every day.

But overall, life is good in the Muntshe pride. There is play, one of a young animal's favourite activities, rumbling their brothers and sisters. They also participate in the hunt, but often watch from afar as the lead lionesses make the kill. On occasions they watch their fathers hunt, eyes fixed on the impressive power and directness when tackling animals.

Movement excites Ufudu. From young, the dark tip on his mum's tail was the source of much fun. Also, the quick movements of squirrels, dwarf mongoose, lizards, ground birds and even larger things like hippo and elephant – but always at a distance with the big things. Anything that moves captures his attention. He also likes to lie on the tar roads where the Muntshe pride lazes on cool nights, enjoying the warmth. The roads are easier to walk on than the veld, even his fathers do so.

The trees nearby the kill, the dead ones without foliage, are full of vultures. The vultures prefer the dead trees because they can easily get going with their large wingspan. A few trees with foliage like the knob thorn and apple-leaf have patient vultures. Under the jackal-berry, it looks like a bomb has gone off. Tawny lions all inert, lying around in the shade, full bellies. One lion's head will lift to check the carcass every few minutes, making sure nothing untoward is happening. Black-backed jackals are tolerated if they keep on the opposite side of the kill. They snipe in, grab and then trot off with a bounce to eat a titbit. The effort of a charge would be too much for such a minimal loss to the lions at this stage.

The carcass emits an aroma, a sickly-sweet metallic smell of blood mingling with meat rot. It is a full twenty-four hours since the bald buffalo died. Flies buzz around and land on the lions. Even when they seem dead to the world, tails flick and ears twitch to get the flies away.

Daytime gives way to night, and the temperature cools. Lions join the carcass, others sleep the deep fitful sleep that a full belly brings. The lead lioness rises and strides towards the water's edge. The lionesses and sub-adults follow. She looks into the water and crouches down. Her tongue extends and folds backwards, the top of her tongue touches the water and she draws it back into her mouth. The papillae hooks on her tongue aid the fluid mechanics in lapping the water. She gets a rhythm going. The lions lie next to each other, drinking together in the moonlight.

Black-mane lifts his head as he hears the lapping. He stares, computing if he is going to join. The drinking continues for minutes, and Black-mane rises and stretches. His full belly swings as he moves towards the others. The lead lioness stops, turns and moves to the carcass.

Young Ufudu bounds after her. He jumps on her flank as he has done countless times before in play. The lead lioness turns angrily and hisses wide-mouthed at him. Insele bounds towards the lead lioness to join in the fun while Timid gazes. Black-mane ambles towards the dam. His jowls move with each heavy step, and he stops, staring with razor-sharp focus. Anger rises, deep-seated anger at the young males. He charges in, rears up on his back feet, and swipes at the young male. Ufudu is unprepared for the vicious charge but jinxes away in reflex, catching only a glancing blow, yet the force is enough to swing him around. The pride erupts in a noise that deafens and reverberates. Squabbles break out, and Blondie and Half-tail charge in too, targeting the young males. The youngsters flop on their backs and show their bellies in submission. The noise lessens, and the growls become roars from Black-mane, as his coalition partners join in. The three male lions roar in unison.

A male lion's roar is 114 decibels. And in perfect conditions in open country, humans can hear them up to eight kilometres away. Lions can hear it from further away with their superior hearing. It's clear what the lions are saying, even to humans. 'This is mine; this is mine, mine, mine, mine, mine.' Many people think a lion's roar is what MGM puts on before a movie. But that's not a roar; that's more of a growl. Some say it is even a tiger growl they use. A lion's roar rises in crescendos that taper into grunts. It is a sound that, if you hear it in the distance, is pleasant, but if it is emitted near you, it can be terrifying. The males mostly roar just before dawn but roars can be heard anytime if the mood or occasion calls for an announcement.

Ufudu is still on his back, perplexed about what he had done wrong. He does not know that his mere existence in the pride is the problem. He stays on his back, confused by his error. He once fed when Black-mane was eating with Half-tail and

Blondie. They even chased the lionesses off and let him and his brothers eat. Black-mane goes towards the water's edge with Blondie and Half-tail. The lioness and her sisters head towards the carcass. Ufudu, Insele, Timid and Jelwana stare at each other in the moonlight for some time and then start grooming each other, forming and sustaining a bond after the trauma.

They're uncertain why they treated so; even the lionesses don't seem to be rooting for them. Ufudu rolls onto his belly and stares towards the lioness as she moves towards the kill. He gets up and follows and finds a place near the ebony jackal-berry trunk and falls asleep.

Some hyenas are getting bolder. In the night, long whoop-like calls are replaced with laugh-like cackles. Hyenas start materialising. Black-mane, Blondie and Half-tail charge them a few times. The hyenas settle in a half-circle twenty metres from the kill. Expectant.

CHAPTER 5

At the dawn of the third day, the sun rises to find the lions starting to move into the brush on the Muntshe hill. Two lioness sub-adults are on the kill. The hyenas are students of body language and see this as an opportunity and edge closer. Their faces are broad, and mouths powerful, stronger jaws than the lion, designed to eat bone and sinew – the tough parts. They send excited giggles into the air as they descend on the kill. The vultures pour from the trees and head down to the carcass, a scrum of spotted hyenas and wings. Some birds and hyenas get into the chest cavity.

The vultures hiss and make a sound you may know already. It was used for some of the dinosaur sounds in Jurassic Park. Throaty sounds like a diesel engine battling to start, coupled with the high-pitched sound of a cordless drill. Hyenas chase one or two vultures off, but more come in and descend into the chaos of the cleaning crew. Some vultures squabble by standing upright and kicking out with their talons. Some land on top of others. Now and then the lions charge them for their instinct compels them to not share. The vultures take off and return when the lions swing their heavy bellies back to the shade.

The vultures can even eat harmful bacteria like anthrax and kill it in their acidic stomachs. They can clean a 100-kilogram wildebeest carcass in half an hour. The already-eaten buffalo carcass lies deflated, a shadow of its former self, but even now, still a reservoir of resources for others. Ribs show and move with the scavengers' efforts. Bald buffalo's once proud boss and horns lie on the ground.

The lions watch the scavengers, but they are sated. They drift in and out of sleep in the shade of trees for the entire day.

In the midday heat, Ufudu gets up and walks towards an adult lioness. He licks her, and a growl emits from under a raisin bush. He ignores it, not understanding that it is directed at him, and licks the lioness again. A tawny streak, as Blondie charges out from the raisin bush, the black-ringed mouth open wide, tail whipping to the side in a warning. With a throaty growl, he hits Ufudu at full speed. He does not bite. The body check of a 200-kilogram lion accelerating knocks Ufudu into the air. Landing on his paws, he bounds away with his tail down and rolls onto his back as Blondie tracks him. Blondie stands over him and swats him twice with his large paws, his claws retracted.

The blows cause Ufudu to wince and his slight mane picks up leaves, sticks and dirt as he submits on the ground. Blondie calms down at this display but stands tall over Ufudu. Watching him, searching for any defiance. The other lions raise their heads to watch this but lose interest and go back to sleep.

Blondie returns to his raisin bush and marks and kicks his legs as he does so. Ufudu rolls onto his belly and growls – a small growl – but he can't restrain it. Blondie turns, and the dust rises in a cloud as his paws dig into the African soil to get traction. Ufudu raises himself on his back legs and tries to swat the blurring Blondie. Blondie does not avoid the blow; he runs into it as if it does not exist and powers through to bite. His canines find fur, but he does not bite as he could; he just holds and shakes. Ufudu is shaken like a rag doll with the power of a dominant force. Blondie lets go, and Ufudu falls and lies on his back again, bleeding from his flank. Blondie is not fooled this time and extends his claws and swipes twice at the face of Ufudu. Fur flies and blood flows. Satisfied, Blondie has reiterated his dominance; he stands over Ufudu and watches. He growls and salivates, waiting for any cheek.

Some lionesses are standing, Black-mane's head is up watching the spectacle, and Half-tail is still asleep. Blondie charges at Jelwana, who sprints away before he rolls on his back and squirms in submission. Blondie scent marks. He sidles up to a brown ivory tree stump, extends his claws, and scratches the bark. Then he stretches and heads to his cool spot under the raisin bush.

The carcass now has new colours near it, white bird droppings and several feathers blowing in the wind. Hyenas have spread the carcass in different directions; a leg goes one way, a rib another. Hyenas get so much calcium in their diet. When a hyena defecates, the scat starts off green in colour, but as it hardens in the African sun, it turns white. Other animals, like the leopard tortoise, will eat the scat to get the calcium their shells need. A multivitamin. If you and I had to touch hyena scat or any predator for that matter, the organisms and bacteria could cause us harm.

Day turns to night. The hippopotamuses leave the water and head off into the pasture grounds to eat vegetation in the cover of darkness. The lions are comfortable in their spots, not compelled to move anywhere. They watch the scavengers move about with heavy eyes. Ufudu is stiff and sore from the tender spot where the buffalo kicked him, and now the scratches on his face that burn and the few puncture marks on his flank. Jelwana, Insele and Timid lick his wounds and groom him. None of the others in the pride do. The youngsters try to sleep too, but they are restless.

With the sunrise, the pride drinks water at the dam. They chase a few vultures, black-backed jackals and hyenas from the water's edge, out of habit. The vultures run; the sub-adult lionesses chase after them with the vigour of youth. The heavy birds run along the ground and flap their wings, the sound is heavy, and they take off in slow motion. The hyenas are experts at giving enough ground to appease the lion but not running off.

The young male lions watch from the Muntshe thickets; they can sense a change. But out of habit, they stretch and follow the others down to the dam. They join the long line of lions lying next to each other on the water's edge and drink. Black-mane drinks longer, then stands, stretches, yawns, walks a few metres, drops his flank, and defecates. The stench of digested meat and blood fills the immediate area. They walk back to the thickets, lie in various places, and sleep again.

The young males play with bones, chase vultures and jackals with energy then come into the shade. A few growls when they come to lie down, but they die down, and the bush sounds take over as the lions slumber. Cicadas buzz, and a Levaillant's cuckoo gives his call. A few human voices drift down from the picnic site above them.

The lead lioness gets up and urinates. Black-mane comes over and takes a deep sniff. He flehmens and downloads the information, and another large lioness also urinates. He strides over and sniffs her urine. The grimace crumples his face, and his eyes become tiny slits. He raises his head side to side as he processes the scent information. The lead lioness watches him. She lies down, but she is restless now. She relaxes for a while, but the feeling grows; she walks up to Black-mane as he lies watching her and lifts her tail and whips it, like a finger saying, 'come here'. She moves her tail in a different direction. He needs no encouragement. The other lioness stretches and does the same, encouraging Black-mane's attention again.

The two lionesses walk away from the pride to the dam flats with their tails flicking. Black-mane starts following them. Blondie stares, rises and stretches, and follows. The other lionesses and sub-adults watch, except for Half-tail, who is fast asleep. The lionesses disappear in the tall grass in front of Black-mane. The scent is like a highway, and Black-mane follows them into the tall red grass.

A Swanson spurfowl alarms and flies from the walking lions. The sky is blue with a few fluffy candy floss clouds. Half-tail wakes and rises with the spurfowl alarm. His mane is tufted with grass, and he walks towards the urine and smells, and grimaces. He looks around but can't see his brothers or the females so he smells the ground to see which direction they have taken.

Timid, the young lion, is fast asleep, and in his way as he tries to find the path. He growls and Timid wakes up to bared yellow canines and Half-tail's hot, stinky breath. He immediately rolls onto his back in submission. Half-tail has lioness-in-oestrus scent in his nostrils and no said lionesses in sight. He bears down on Timid, who squirms and wiggles on his back. Jelwana gets up to flee, and Half-tail leaves Timid and charges at him. The ground shakes with the growls and dust sprays into the sunlight. Half-tail is furious. Jelwana sprints as briskly as his legs can pump. Half-tail's frustrations zone in on him. He bounds towards the dam, after Jelwana. His mane is blowing windswept as he moves forward. Muscles pump and strain, and he catches Jelwana and clips his rear leg. Jelwana rolls in the dust. Ufudu streaks out. Half-tail spins and locks onto the movement and bounds after Ufudu. Insele bolts too; they melt into the grass and do not stop. Grass spikes and tufts tear at them. Jelwana rolls in the dirt as he trips but lands on his feet and heads towards the grass. Timid slinks into the foliage where he is. Half-tail sprints after the fleeing Jelwana and Ufudu.

Then a scent hits his nose, and he skids to a stop. He circles and sniffs, putting his muzzle near to the ground. He inhales... youngsters forgotten, his rage dissipates. He trails the scent left by the lionesses in oestrus and his brothers. The young males keep running, unsure what Half-tail's location is. In the last few days the beatings have intensified. The lionesses are not including them in the grooming.

Insele and Ufudu slacken after some time. They come to a single knob thorn tree and halt under it, panting in the shade. A tawny eagle is in the branches and stares down at the two lions beneath him. A soft contact call filters through the bush and they recognise it as Jelwana. They contact call chuff back, and Jelwana emerges from the grass with his head down. The brothers rub heads together and give soft encouraging vocalisations. Jelwana lies down, and they pant and begin to relax.

But any movement grabs their attention now. A blue-headed lizard moves over the bark of the knob thorn, and they all stare up. The tawny flies off to catch the rising thermals from the baked African soil, and the sound of his departure causes them to startle. The vultures are rising in circles into the blue sky on these thermals. Like glider pilots, they circle higher. Some break off to the right at a certain height and start circling again and the young lions stare up at them. The adrenaline eventually wears off, and they fall asleep.

Jelwana hears the contact call from his slumber. He opens his eyes and moves his ears to cup in the direction. Listening with these adjustments, he hears it again, louder. He knows who that is, he responds, and Timid appears out of the blue buffalo grass. Timid rubs each of his compatriot's faces, and they lie on and with and by each other – a jumble of touching limbs. They instinctively know they are alone now. They can't look back, only forward. They can't stay at Muntshe pride lands. It's time to pave their own way.

Night falls, and they hear the Muntshe pride roaring to the north. They listen to the echoes of the past as wave after wave of sound moves over them. They can recognise the individuals, hear them, and know who is announcing themselves, they even know how many are roaring at a time. They shift around and groom each other, reaffirming bonds and their decisions.

Timid stares back at where the roars came from. He turns and looks at his brothers lying at different angles. He sneezes, sighs and flops down, and tries to go back to sleep.

The circle of Muntshe continues as it always has here in Africa.

CHAPTER 6

The four young lions rest. Blondie, Half-tail, and Black-mane roar. Sometimes the Muntshe lionesses join in. The young lions do not respond. They rise at noon and head south.

The grass is thick, and they struggle until they get to a dirt road. The S29 dirt road is a boundary road for the Muntshe lion pride. Easy to walk and scent mark along a spacious road, and out of habit, they walk east. The scent of the southern pride marking their northern boundary present. Sometimes the Muntshes push a little into this neighbour's territory. Occasionally the southern pride had pushed a little north. Pushing into the fringes of the territory where lion prides overlap – buffer zones. The core of the territory is defended with tooth and claw, but little forays into the fringes are tolerated. Fringe raids, if caught, result more in theatrics than action. But never venture into the heartland of the territory, unless you want war. Because it would be a war declaration.

The youngsters know this but are left with little choice. Blondie, Black-mane, and Half-tail control the southern pride too. They come and go as they want. This is not an option for the youngsters though, as dispersed young male lions are 'animal non grata' with other lions unless they meet other young males who have been dispersed. Young males that find each other during dispersal can form coalitions with bonds that cement them just as strongly as if they were blood brothers. Another option they have is to take over a pride, but this is not yet possible.

Jelwana has detected a whiff of one of his fathers. He scrapes over it, which is easy to do when they are not watching. Roaming is effortless on the wide-open natural space of the road. They play, chase and enjoy each other, until they hear wheels on washboard ruts, and they turn around as a car approaches. and halts twenty metres from them.

Ufudu, Insele, Timid and Jelwana gaze at the occupants with their mouths open. The tourists return the favour. The lions have seen many cars, but it is strange without pride lionesses nearby. They are interested but nervous, they lie down with their bellies on the dirt road and their heads up. Three black and white, long-tailed magpie shrikes glide above them. All gaze up at the same time to track the movement. One of the car's occupants giggles, and Timid takes fright and hides in the grass. Jelwana, Ufudu and Insele ogle the car. Their heads make little side motions to track movement. They lift their noses and sniff.

The impasse ends with the lions losing interest in the stationary car, getting up, and walking east. The car's engine starts and frightens them, and they jog on the road. Timid follows from the grass and strides after his brothers, jumping on their back legs. They envelop him, rumble, and play, much to the tourists' delight. Camera shutters click as the young lions wrestle on the road, using the movements similar to those the Muntshes utilised against the bald buffalo. Timid is mobbed, and he growls a tiny growl and then slaps Jelwana. Ufudu is still tender, a flinch of pain shudders through him when they smash into his flanks.

Another car, a low sedan, joins the sighting behind the first vehicle. The initial car moves to the left, considerate of the second vehicle's line of sight. The tourist in the low sedan glides his car on the right side. Two wheels park on the tall yellow thatching grass on the verge and the smell of crushed grass permeates the air. The driver is making frantic movements and the occupants of the first car gawk at him. His hands disappear to the passenger seat and he grabs a bulky camera and long lens. The camera lens has a camouflaged military print cover. Opening his sunroof, he stands stiffly on his front seat as it squeals and squeaks in protest, and peers out from above his roof through the opening. Placing the camera to his cheek, he gazes down the viewfinder. His exposure is good, and he half depresses the shutter on a focal point he has put on Timid's nose. It sharpens, and he clicks, releasing the shutter and taking a picture of the scene. He smiles and grunts and loses his footing, his knee hitting the hooter.

All four lions stop their play and turn towards the threatening sound. It blares like a troubled elephant trumpeting. They see a human form levitating out of the top of the car with a large object in his hands. With an alarmed chuff, they run into the grasslands.

Insele, Jelwana, Timid and Ufudu hear the people shouting angrily at each other and keep their heads down in the long grass. A few more hoots and noises, they hide lower. A car drives away, and the noises diminish. One car still tries to locate them and drives up and down, up and down. In the shade of the grass, they drift off into slumber and eventually the other car leaves.

They wake later when the sun is lower and behind them, and set off on the road again, walking east. They come to the S122 and S29 junction, turn north, and lope up the S122 road in Muntshe lion territory, away from the immediate vicinity of the pride and the dominant male lions, but still a familiar area.

They head north along the road, and a marula tree spreads a crown-shaped dome of shade next to the road on the left. Its bark is a silver grey – a line of bark stripped off until the heart-wood on the east side. An elephant has stripped the cambium layer for its nutrients in the dry months. Despite this disability, the marula clings to life, and spreads its shade. The shade is inviting; they lie under it and drift off to sleep. Marula fruits lie hard and green spread over the base and Timid paws and chews on a few during his regular security checks. Muntshe Mountain rises on the west, and the Lebombo on the east.

Thirst wakes them before sunset. Smelling the air for any water, they move to the north. A mud wallow that started as an elephant footprint was enlarged and expanded by a warthog's enthusiasm, grown by the animals' rumps until it became a big enough water trap for the buffalo and elephant to wallow in. Now it houses water for the young lions, empty of large visible bioengineers. All four lie touching each other, shoulder to shoulder as they lap up the orange mud-filled water.

The lions walk to a nearby sjambok pod tree that sprouts from a termite mound. The soil of the disused mound is packed hard and elevated. Jelwana lowers into a crouch and defecates. Timid watches and joins in. The smell of a carnivore's scat is better experienced written. They lie under the sjambok pod tree, so named because its pods are long and cylindrical, resembling the whip known in South Africa as the sjambok. The soil on the termite mound is concrete-like and cool in the shade. Elevated so a slight breeze finds them prone.

They yawn widely, increasing the oxygen to their brains. It must be dawning on them that meals are now their responsibility but their tummies have enough buffalo in them for this not to be an immediate problem. They stop yawning, spawl and fall asleep.

Sunset brings the soothing call of the nocturnal fiery-necked nightjar. The stars deepen and set, and the four lions sleep. Now and then, a head will raise as they scan the area for any potential danger, not least Blondie, Black-mane, and Half-tail. They hear the Muntshe pride roaring. Tonight, in the distance they can hear the southern pride too, responding. They sit up and listen to the announcements, which taper off, and the fiery-necked nightjar continues. An anvil-shaped, tall cumulonimbus cloud flashes lightning over the plains. The sound of thunder rumbles, and the wind picks up and gusts. The lions huddle together and eye the fireworks. They have never experienced a storm before without a pride. The rain pelts them and then moves along the grasslands.

Damp and awake before sunrise, they distort themselves in stretches, give cavernous yawns and head north along the S122 road. The road is effortless for them to follow with their night vision. Walking along, decoding the Muntshe pride marks, they romp together. A common duiker bursts from cover before them and dives into the grass, too fast for the lions to show any interest other than surprise. They stalk each other, wrestle, cavort and stroll north, tails in an upheld C position, flicking the dark end, communicating that they are walking here.

Stomach reverberations of an elephant breeding herd are emitted ahead. The lions sit on their rumps and wait for them to pass. An elephant cow pulls tufts of grass out with her trunk, shakes off the soil and places them in her mouth. Young elephants are kept safely near the middle of the herd or next to their mums. In the past when with the pride, the young lions would show themselves and have the confidence to cause an uproar. Rumbles and trumpets would sound as the elephants encircled their young and faced the lions. Some would open their large ears, tuck their trunks in and charge out at them, kicking dust at the tawny cats who would retreat at speed. But alone like this, this compulsion to make trouble does not arise.

They watch from afar as a large cow raises her trunk and stops to smell the air. Their aroma carries, for her tail stiffens and moves to the side, rigid. She emits a deep rumbling command, and the young elephants rush into the middle, and the cows encircle them in a protective ring facing outwards. The cows raise their trunks and widen their ears to make themselves look bigger. They are the world's largest land mammals so it seems unnecessary. The elephant cows move their heads from side to side and one trumpets. Her trunk snakes into an upwards position like a periscope and the trunk opening flares and moves around sniffing in different directions, trying to glean where the smell emanates from. The youngsters mill around in the centre emulating their guardians. The very young elephants can't control their trunks and they wiggle and flap on their face. The lions leer.

After a few minutes, the matriarch seems satisfied and issues an order. She could be specific and use a herd member's name, yes… latest studies using artificial intelligence have shown that elephants use individual names. This, however, is a general command for all. Together they file off the road in a tight grey column and head west towards Muntshe, silent for such large animals. Kilometres away, another breeding herd picks up the seismic movements from their rumbles on their toenails, the vibrations move up their skeletal system into their inner ear and they hear the all-clear order too.

The lions observe them go, then continue down the road northwards. Light rises above the Lebombo to the east, a new day's dawn. Grey go-away birds shout their rude call. The large ground hornbill with the large red throat patch calls and the first few notes fool Ufudu. He thinks it is a lion, but he realises his mistake and they continue ambling, stopping to dispose of the digested buffalo at regular intervals until their stomachs are no longer distended.

A tree squirrel emits a frantic alarm as he sees the lions strolling up the road. His tail whips with each syllable of warning. From the safety of a marula, he is brave. The lions peer up at him and his display. A kudu barks at them as they stroll.

Coming across a water hole they lie down a few hundred metres from it in the grass hoping something will come to drink. Nothing does; the kudu and the squirrel have called a warning that other creatures heed. Lazily they head north as the sun sets. Now their stomachs are twinging the first receptors of hunger. They move with eyes roaming in front, and they often look behind them, assessing the air and listening for movement.

CHAPTER 7

Daylight finds them lying on the road sleeping, and a tourist car spots them mid-morning. Prone, looking up at the tourists, they roll over and go back to sleep. The tourist car loses interest in the lazy cats and drives on the verge through the grass past them. Jelwana watches the spinning wheels, rises, and gives the rubber a swipe… the car stops. His interest dissipates. The car starts and drives off. They laze about until it gets too hot and head for shade, restlessness in their bones. Their bowels rumble, and they gaze at each other, heavy heave panting.

Night falls, and they head north on the S122. Jelwana hears the sound first. Moving off the road into the grass, cupping his ears in the direction he senses it. Ufudu, Insele and Timid shadow him. He hears it again and crouches, and the others emulate his movements, stalking through the grass towards the slight sound, his night vision straining to see.

An opening in the grass in front of him. His pupils widen, and starlight comes through his eyes without encumbrance and the mirror behind his retina bounces it back a second time for capture emphasis. Circular grass is bent to the side. Crawling forward he sees a neck periscoping up from the grass with large open eyes. Jelwana freezes. Glaring into the ostrich's eyes, he is unaware that the ostrich is fast asleep with its eyes open. He gathers himself soundlessly and launches at the flightless bird, Jelwana pounces and Insele, Timid and Ufudu rush in. Their collective weight and suddenness go the lions' way before the ostrich even realises he is dead.

The blood of independence drips down their throats for the first time. They quarrel for a piece of real estate and gorge. Feathers fly into the night sky as the young lions devour and tear into their spoil. They spit and growl at each other and swipe each other's noses. Calming, they lie beside their prize in the night-time, no longer hungry, grooming and licking each other in the way of apology.

Black-mane roars in the distance and Blondie and Half-tail join in. The young lions will have to venture out into the unknown. If they follow this road, they might bump into the three large males on a territorial patrol. And they cannot have that.

So, in the morning, after they finish the scraps of the ostrich, they head due east away from the Muntshe pride towards the Lebombo rhyolite mountains that rise like a wave in the east. Into the unfamiliar scents of a foreign lion. Instinctively, they know they are dead if another dominant lion finds them. Another pride will not welcome them. They are not of age or mature; they do not have the body size and the gravitas a dominant male lion needs to protect their territory. Their tests and education are still pending, in the wind, the air they breathe, and the soil they walk on. A life unencumbered, but the potential for tragedy around every corner.

They head east, cautious, stopping and listening, smelling for any new signs of other lions. Trying to avoid them at all costs.

Days turn into weeks, and they no longer hear the Muntshe pride. They hear other lions, which is frightening. They do not scent mark and move from the roars, trying to keep their distance in a high-stakes hide-and-seek game. They do not vocalise other than soft contact call amongst themselves. But they must eat and have managed to scrounge a few small meals that have kept them sustained but hungry. They are lean and growing, like awkward teenagers. Their limbs are thin, energy fluctuates, and they need a substantial meal.

They observe vultures descending in the distance, indicating a kill, but they are invading the land of another pride – perhaps feasting there now – and are not yet desperate enough to be that foolish. They have picked up the scent of another cat, a solitary one, a leopard and they are following it in the hopes of scrounging a meal. But the leopard is too bush-smart for the youngsters and has evaded them. They had stalked and missed a kudu cow the previous day. Hunting was proving far more complicated without lionesses.

And they lie despondently under an evergreen magic guarri tree in the shade. Resting and napping in the heat.

Insects buzz and the lions pant, until suddenly there is silence. And the four lions' heads rise with their ears cupped to ascertain why. A red-faced Swanson's spurfowl sudden alarm splits the air and the youngsters stare towards the sound with intensity, no longer panting.

Before they can even get to their feet, a male lion with a dark mane streaks in from the long grass, huge sharp canines dominate his thirty teeth which he displays in a cavernous gape. The ferocious jaws grab Timid and secure him with one powerful bite. Growling, with his quarry secure, the large-maned dominant lion with quivering muscles and flying spit slashes at Timid. Not trying to disperse sons – this lion's mindset is killing intruders.

Timid utters a powerful growl and tries to turn and hit out with his forepaws, but can't. He tries to rake with his rear paws but his efforts are useless. The power gripping him is unlike anything he has experienced. Another male lion rushes in, grabs Timid's belly, and bites down, swiping paws with claws out. Fur flies and blood splatters onto the African soil. Timid's growls decrease.

Jelwana, Ufudu and Insele run for their lives. Any idea of fighting for Timid vanished with a huge third lion rushing in and grabbing Timid's throat. The unexpected attack has them overawed and rattled, racing away like impala from the ambush.

Timid's mouth closes, and his eyes glaze over. The sun reflects in his eyes as he sighs for the last time.

A fourth male lion emerges from the bush and chases the departing youngsters. He slides to a stop and turns around at the growls and commotion under the magic guarri bush. Timid's blood seeps out into the ground, into the soil, and down into the earth. The dominant lions worry the carcass but do not consume it. Now and then, they growl at it and swipe it again and bite the lifeless young lion. Tiring, they lie down under the magic guarri next to Timid's body, happy that they have dispersed the intruders and protected their territory. They will patrol in the direction the other males ran.

Insele, Jelwana and Ufudu cannot maintain the frantic pace they are fleeing at and slow down to a trot. Mouths hang open and suck in air as they turn around and listen, to sense any pursuers. They don't rest the entire day and night but head south. In shock, they hear the roars of the male lions behind them at night and the pride to their east, now far behind. They have barely survived their first test. A few weeks into independence, they are one down.

Timid is eaten by hyenas and spread out over the savanna. A leopard tortoise indirectly eats some of Timid, by way of hyena scat, craving the bone-rich hyena's dropping which provide calcium for its shell. At the same time, a giraffe bends down at Mlondozi and picks up a bone from bald buffalo that the hyenas did not eat. He sucks on it for the nutrients his massive skeletal structure demands.

CHAPTER 8

T he young males walk, weary and frantic. A red-faced Swanson spurfowl bursts from the underbrush into the air with a warning call. All three lions jump with fright as a steenbok breaks its stoic statue stance and bolts from them. The young lions flee, rattled. But they are learning a vital lesson of vigilance.

They finally come to a large river – the Sabie River. The name of this river is derived from the Swazi word Ulsaba which means fear. Apt for the young male lions' current demeanour. It has many crocs and hippos and the territories of large cats border this river. It is flowing swiftly as it is summer, the rainy season. They stare at the broad swirling brown river, walking along the bank to see if there are any natural bridges over the river. Sycamore figs cling to the riverbank with yellowish bark and thick canopies. Trumpeter hornbills feast on the figs and give their horn-like call. Grey vervet monkeys stare down from a large sausage tree, with fruit like hanging salami sausages, lithe among the branches. The males have testicles in a shade that is an unmistakable bright neon blue, which gives blue balls a different meaning. Glaring at the lions and sounding the alarm, they jump from branch to branch moving their heads from side to side, but knowing they are safe from the tawny cats. The vervets would be apoplectic if they were orange with rosettes, for the leopard is agile enough to catch a monkey in the trees.

A rattling cisticola bird begins cautioning from the grass banks at the three lions striding into the cool reception; understandably – you cannot expect the food to love you. Their tails are all in a C position, and the black marking on the tip flicks forward and backwards, communicating that they are walking, not stalking. An African fish eagle takes off from a large matumi tree. A Verreaux eagle-owl with pink eyelids goggles from an apple-leaf tree – named apple-leaf not because it produces an apple-like fruit. Rather, it has large round leaves and in the dry season the desiccated leaves fall to the ground and when you walk under the tree, each step sounds like you are taking a bite of an apple as you crunch the leaves underfoot.

A bushbuck ram surveys the vervets and sees the lions. He barks, his body language rigid. A herd of impala, the dainty, rust-coloured antelope, with big bright eyes, startle. The word antelope, some propose, comes from the Greek 'anthos' for flower, and ops for 'eye', perhaps meaning 'beautiful eye'. It's likely to be romantic etymology, but regardless, they do have lovely eyes. The animals have legs that look like they should snap without effort but are nimble and agile. Only the male buck have horns, which are long, slender, strongly ridged and lyre-shaped. They stare towards the lions and shout an alarm, which sounds like a foot scuffing a dirt road. The sound crescendos as the lions come closer, but as they walk past, it dwindles.

You can follow the lions' progress through this riverine area with the alarm calls. Nature is warning of their presence. A leopard languishing on an ebony jackal-berry tree on the opposite side of the river opens her blue eyes. Staring towards the three lions walking on the opposite side, she yawns a few times. She calls a raspy call, not the wood sawing territory sound, but a contact call for her cub, playing on the ground. She listens for him to heed, but he does not, so she calls again. The cub bounds up the tree at the second call, a little ball of fur so fuzzy at this size that he looks out of focus and not pin sharp. He is eight weeks old and climbs up the dark bark to his mum, where she grooms him. The cub is all energy, looking in different directions, his movements fast, kitten-like. Bounding higher up in the tree, he watches the leaves move in the wind. Satisfied, the mother leopardess goes back to sleep.

A kudu bellows from the riverbank at the lions strolling along one of the most predator-rich real estates. At times it sounds like the entire animal kingdom is swearing at them. Yet no other lions see them. Sometimes you are fortunate, and young dispersing lions need acres of fortune.

They stride along and observe a bridge, a bridge over the Sabie River, a bridge built on top of a causeway. It has a fish run to allow the fish to ladder up on the southern side of the riverbank. The Sabie is pouring under this mid-level bridge. Hippopotamuses languish at the top in the deeper water, yawning and displaying their impressive teeth, canines that can reach forty-five centimetres. Sandbank islands in the river have large crocodiles basking in the sun. They have lots of teeth and lie with their mouths open, regulating their body temperature.

The three lions stop and peer because at least six cars are on the bridge gawking at the wildlife. They recline under the dense shade of a Natal mahogany tree with deep, dark, tennis court green leaves, and they scan the bridge. A vehicle with no sides and a canvas roof is looking with binoculars in their direction. A nature guide hearing the alarm calls is glassing the banks. He cannot find the lions in the shade behind the shrubs and grass; they can see him and his frustration. If Kruger tourists, and even the professional guides that traverse here daily and call this their office, knew how many animals they couldn't see, depression would set in. The nature guide drives off after a few minutes, unaware, and the bush sounds return to the chirp of insects and bird calls, and the alarm calls cease.

The lions can see a large structure up the river with humans sitting on it – it's the Lower Sabie rest camp's Mugg & Bean deck restaurant. The traffic on the bridge disperses, with only one car left. The lions rise and saunter toward the H10 road, emerging from the grass and strolling on the road over the bridge. The car begins to drive forward but stalls in excitement as the three lions stride over the bridge, tails in the air.

Other cars arrive. Even the sound of the river running is not enough to drown the vervet monkeys' alarms which have begun again. A baboon adds his bark to the mix. The lions halt at the baboon's bark and stare at the troop bounding up an umbrella thorn acacia that hugs the northern bank of the Sabie River. The primates stand rigid on the tree branches and yelp loud warnings. The lions gaze up at their theatrics and then continue. The sightseers in the initial tourist car smile as the three lions stride past them while others strain to see past the traffic jam on the bridge.

The Sabie River is teeming with birds. A hippo snorts as a Goliath heron fishes the fish ladder run. A grey heron surfs the back of a hippo in the deeper water, fishing from his private pontoon. The lions bumble over the bridge past the vibrant Red Bishop on the reeds. The southern masked weavers build their nests, and the wagtails scurry from the lion. The pied kingfishers that hunt from the bridge fly a small circle away and land again behind the lion, watching them pass. A hamerkop is frogging in the marshlands near the fish run. A waterbuck with an impressive sweep of horns leers at the lions, rigid, but comfortable with the distance.

CHAPTER 9

The lions bound up the southern bank of the Sabie River and over the H4-2 road into dense sickle bush thickets on the southern side of the tar road, leaving the river of fear conquered.

If they had peered back from the northern side, they would have been able to see Muntshe Mountain or even from the southern side of the bank of the Sabie River. But they don't. They saunter through the sickle bush for kilometres, instinctively realising the noise they attracted along the dense riverine area is a liability. They move a bit further, into an area with less game, thus fewer predators. Comfortable with the distance, they find a weeping boer-bean tree and laze under it, grooming each other and nuzzling their heads together, forging their bond. They drift into the fitful stop-start sleep of a wild animal living a wild life. Times are getting desperate for a meal but they are lethargic after the constant upheaval since Timid met his demise.

Then a musty earth smell assaults their nostrils and raising their heads in unison they see a bull elephant nearby. He carries his head high and sways from side to side in time with his paces. The temporal gland on his face is streaming and his penis sheath dribbles and stains green from the constant moisture. Urine spills onto his back legs marking them dark.

He is in musth – a testosterone-laden condition which floods his body with androgenic hormones. It makes some bulls aggressive. The lions have smelt it before and it smells like trouble – even to virgin nostrils. The elephant flares his ears, and his stomach rumbles as he picks up the lions' scent. He gives a sharp trumpet and lifts his huge head with all the creases and folds a pachyderm possesses. He shakes his head in irritation, his large ears clap with the momentum, and the sound carries towards the young lions who shift uncomfortably with this display.

The elephant turns sideways to them and it seems he might be striding away but then he faces the lions and lifts his trunk high like a periscope scenting them. He drops his trunk and shakes his head again, crabbing sideways. His trunk twists and turns and settles over one tusk as he ascertains where the scent is coming from. Finally, he spots the three lions looking at him fifty metres away under the weeping boer-bean. He halts and gazes, he picks his front left foot up and swings it in the air as he processes what he is seeing, and he places it down and shakes his head in irritation.

The lions stir a bit but do not bolt away, they stare with intense interest, their heads erect and their ears cupped in the direction of the elephant. The bull walks rapidly with his head high, ears wide and trunk tucked in, hurrying straight for the boer-bean. Lions disperse. The elephant skids to a halt, vocalises and trumpets, and kicks dust. He spins his tall frame in different directions as the cats give way. Satisfied with the respect the lions have given him, he trumpets one piercing time and then walks hastily with a stiff tail towards the horizon. Either to a cow elephant in oestrus, a marula tree full of fruits, or food that he fancies. Whatever he finds first.

The lions head back to the shade of the tree but are uneasy, so they continue south. Hitting the S82 sand road makes the going easier, but they're nervous. The road feels revealing; they are gleaning scents that tell them this is the territory of another lion pride. They move east into the sickle bush thickets, avoiding the scent boundaries.

The sun sets, but the rank odours of the lion pride on the road compel them to continue east. It's a full moon, and they can see the path easily with their night vision-designed eyes. During this time their natal pride would not hunt, as the full moon allows the prey to see them easily at night too. In the distance, they hear a loud booming sound like a thunderstorm, but shorter. They stop and train their cone-shaped ears in the direction the sound echoes. Hearing a thud, they are drawn in that direction. This is not an animal in difficulty, but curiosity pulls the cats. The sounds become clearer as they approach the area where the sound is emanating from. The surrounding bush is quiet. A sodic site is before them, clear of dense vegetation due to the sodium-rich soil found here.

The scent of blood fills their nostrils, hunger speaks, and they bolt into the clearing. The smell of man's sweat assaults their senses. Searching and scanning they find no man as another unfamiliar scent burns their nostrils with its sharpness. A human vocalisation is heard in the distance, and another even further away, as people flee.

JONATHAN COUZENS

A large form lies on its side. It is a rhino, breathing and gurgling, its ears moving side to side unable to move, struggling feebly. It does not look like a rhino as its horns are missing. Blood seeps from where they would usually be. It gurgles. They take a few steps closer and cannot believe their windfall; the rhino ceases breathing as they watch. A huge bull white rhino. Gaping wounds on the shoulder, its chest not rising.

The lions keep looking up and around, trying to glean where the humans are. They cannot pick up any other predator's smell, and it's night, so no vultures. It seems too good to be true, and they pace around the carcass. After a few minutes of staring slack-jawed, the nervous energy dissipates, and the burning hunger drives them. They start at the existing wounds and gorge. They do not clash; there is enough to go around; this is a 2000-kilogram animal.

The next morning they wake up under a sandpaper raisin bush near the sodic site with full bellies and the rising sun. A hyena on patrol worried them late last night, and sent out his laughing call. A clan of twelve adult spotted hyenas heeded the call and arrived in dribs and drabs. The three young lions contemplate, as the carcass belongs to the hyenas now. They cannot dominate against these odds. The hyenas are charging and laughing at them, they retaliate, but it is futile.

Eventually, they swing their heavy bellies to the east as the vultures descend.

CHAPTER 10

A few hours later, Insele, Ufudu and Jelwana whip around as distant roars crash over them. Unbeknownst to them, a male lion with a smudge on his muzzle has been tracking them from the rhino carcass, his muzzle down to the dirt, sniffing the scent that remains like a highway for him to follow. The name humans have bestowed on him is Smudge. He and his brother are under pressure, their range has shrunk and they have retreated south into territory that ends near the H4-2. Smudge halts at the boundary but roars towards the departing scent of the unwelcome lions before he turns back to the carcass.

They dash east, away from the roars, arriving at an area sprouting multi-stemmed false-thorn thickets. They cross over the S130 Gomodwane dirt road near a dead leadwood that stands sentinel in the middle of the road. A large open marshland is here, with pools of water, and the lions need rest. They move to the shade of the multi-stemmed false-thorn trees which encircle the open marshland. Spying towards the west, nothing stirs, and they fall asleep with full bellies as night descends.

A male leopard patrols the road in the distance. They pretend they don't see it. Night becomes day. They drink water and sleep the entire day. Now and then, they look to the west. Their hideout has open ground from that direction; if a male lion comes, they will surely see it. They spend three days in this state of slumber, rest and anxiety.

In the late afternoon, their stomachs compel them to move, and they start strolling south. The sun is losing its venom. They hear a high-pitched noise while walking in the false-thorn thickets – a continuous crescendo of excited high-pitched calls. Recognising the sound, they race towards it, knowing it is a meal for the taking. They streak past shrubs and motor through grass, coming upon white tails sweeping the air, and wide mouths grabbing bits and pieces of an adolescent kudu cow. Pulling in every direction. Mottled white, golden and black wild canids with large round ears and mouths.

The lions race in. The wild dogs scatter, and the kudu falls. Ufudu grabs the bulk of kudu and growls over it and Insele marches after the dogs who spin, whine, and turn, all the while keeping up the high-pitched echo through the African sky. One dog has the rear leg of the kudu in its mouth, and it tries to swallow as much as it can. Other dogs seek to get back their hard-won meal, encouraged by the alpha male and female. Insele and Jelwana join Ufudu. The wild dogs complain and strive to hinder them, racing in and out, whining and talking with their high-pitched squeals. Making themselves a nuisance until the futility of it sinks in and the canids drift off with their springy step and disappear in the tickets.

A lone hyena is drawn by the noise of the conflict. With his knowledgeable eye, he realises this meal will not last. Nor is it worth calling his compatriots; he will sit tight until the lions finish, reclining, watching the youngsters devour their loot. The lions eat their fill, night falls, and they get up and walk further south. Instinctively they realise hanging around meals where there was noise and drama would be unwise. The hyena commandeers the abandoned carcass and crunches through sinew and bones.

The lions move until they come to an open pan, spread in a clearing and fall asleep under the stars. Orion's belt drifts over their heads as the world circles. A lion roars but not in the immediate vicinity and water is abundant in various mud holes in the veld. They remain near one with shade and water for days, licking and grooming themselves of kudu blood.

The pride roars closer, and they move east. Moving at night, the lions do not vocalise beyond the soft contact calls amongst themselves. The false-thorn thickets open to red and yellow thatching grass, grasslands that remind of once-home terri-tory. During the night, Jelwana senses something in the grass. He crouches, stalks and grabs a scrub hare. This hare is only a one-lion meal, so a battle erupts amongst the coalition. Claws flash on faces, and noses split. Whilst they are disagreeing, a jackal appears and steals the hare. Ufudu tries to scamper after the jackal, but his theft has been well calculated and it is in vain. The three brothers calm, compose and preen each other.

They continue to head east and come across the S28 road where they startle a lone lioness. She is strolling along the road, and when Ufudu steps onto it, she halts, stares. When Insele and Jelwana appear, she melts into the tall grass, turning back around, due west for the thickets. A place they had not encountered any other lion yet.

They enter the thickets to smell that a pride of lions had marked their territory while they were in the grasslands. They can smell where the pride picked up their scent and gathered before making the decision to move on. The youngsters are wary and spend a fitful day in the thickets.

When night falls, they beeline in the opposite direction the pride is heading. Moving south. They are ravenous. The breeze comes from the south so their scent wafts behind them, and potential prey cannot smell them.

They come across a breeding herd of impala, lambs are abundant. In Southern Africa, impala have a set rutting and breeding season. The impala rams' testosterone increases with the shortening days of winter, creating a rutting season in winter. After gestation, the lambs drop as a collective in mid-November, in summer as the rains start so the ewes have access to abundant green food to provide milk for the lambs.

Near the equator in areas like East Africa, the rams do not have a set rut time. The days do not shorten on the equator, and the females give birth throughout the year in a staggered fashion which is best for their equator climate.

The abundant lambs in Southern Africa are kept in a creche in the middle of the herd as instinctive protection against predators. The lambs can walk a few minutes after birth and sprint before the end of their first day on earth. They are not helpless, but they lack the adults' guile. Lions and leopards of Southern Africa benefit in two ways because of this: during the rut, distracted males are easier to catch, and now in summer, the youngsters are easy meals. The impala has not smelt them, and they crouch down and manoeuvre as close as possible, keeping as low as they can and crawling along on their bellies.

Their tactic is to charge after one lamb each, and all have their own meal. The impala herd grazes and browses as mixed feeders. Facing in different directions, the herd is tight as it is night and close proximity serves as protection. The lions stalk to ten metres from the fringes of the impala herd, patient. Their muscles contract and vibrate, and the impala fills their vision.

Then as a collective, they burst out. Impala bomb blast in every direction, angle, and height, and not one clashes with another. They snort their warnings at the same time. Some impalas go top right, some bottom left, and everywhere impala scatter. It looks like the shrapnel of a hand grenade detonation as impala blast in different directions. The young lions do not know which one to follow, and in their confusion, they miss them all.

The creche is gone. The impalas run and stop and turn and shout their displeasure. The lions lie down, panting and grooming. They sleep for some time, disturbed only when a hyena comes to investigate the reason for the alarm, but seeing no meal, it disappears at a loping run. The hunger grows, so they force themselves to walk on searching for food. Although they hear and smell options, they cannot capitalise on any of them.

The sun ascends with them still hungry, and finding some shade, the lions snooze, paws in the air and kicking, possibly dreaming of happy hunting grounds.

CHAPTER 11

I n the afternoon, they set off again south, the wind blows towards their faces. A herd of giraffes are in the distance, but only adult lions could pull that off; it's far too challenging as prey for the youngsters. They stroll for kilometres through the night, lying down occasionally but battling to sleep during the day as their stomachs now dictate that they need a meal.

They rise in the day's heat and stumble about, their heads low. It is too hot for a walk so they laze by a mud wallow under a knob thorn tree.

The scent hits their nostrils, and they peer up. A fresh impala kill in the tree stares lifelessly down towards them. The leopard is unseen, but his handiwork is mere metres above them. They stare up, looking at every angle of the straight tree, covered in sharp little hooked thorns on the end of the knobs. The impala is hanging on the first fork of the tree about six metres up. On one side of the fork, his head and leg bulge out, tongue lolling from his mouth and on the other side, legs and rump face down. Wedged tight. The leopard must have seen the three ignorant lions approach whilst at the water and slunk off, discretion the better part of valour.

The three lions stare up into the tree and circle it, hungry for a solution. They have climbed trees before but with a gentle slope and easy climbs, not technical ones. Jelwana is the first to try to explode up the trunk. As his claws dislodge bark, he tries to lever himself up but loses grip and falls. He bounds upright and stares at the impala sticking its tongue out. Ufudu reaches up into the vegetation, extending his front legs, inching until he is standing stretched on his back legs against the tree trunk. His forepaws are in the position used when scratch marking. He hops and tries to get his back leg paws to gain traction. He trips and plummets onto Jelwana, who does not appreciate the head bashing. They growl and scuffle. Insele gazes up, takes a bound and latches on, then inches up like an inchworm. Awkward, bark falls, and painful thorns rip his fur, but up he manoeuvres, ascending the side where the impala's face hangs over. Ufudu endeavours to climb again and strikes his brother. This dislodges him, and both clamour down. They wrestle and growl and spit at each other.

Basking after extending themselves during the brawl they have a snooze, on occasion staring up. A tawny eagle lands on a branch and pecks at the impala. The noise wakes the boys and proves too much; they circle growling at the indifferent bird of prey. They lunge and try to reach but fall short until their gymnastics tire them, and they have another snooze.

When they awake, the tawny eagle has been joined by a bateleur eagle. Insele launches onto the trunk again and inches his way up, little by little. As he nears, Ufudu gets concerned that Insele is going to eat without him, and he tries to grab Insele's rump. Insele is too high for his jealous brother. He clings to the wood as his two brothers pounce, fall, and expend energy. He growls and voices his disdain at his siblings and waits, clinging to the bark till they calm, then inches up further. The two birds of prey glide away.

Insele anchors his front left claws in the bark, making sure his back legs are secure. He lifts and releases one rear paw, anchors it firmly, and ascends. Stretching with one forepaw to grip the impala, he surrenders his rear legs, swinging from the impala head. It does not budge. In a show of strength, he lifts himself with one paw and sinks the claws of his left paw into the impala's neck, now pivoting from both forepaws from the impala carcass. His rear legs hang free and kick with the effort, and he swivels into the knob thorn tree trunk. He growls with the impact, and swiftly adjusts, leveraging his body weight and employing powerful leg kicks.

His agile movements stimulate his brothers, increasing their excitement as the aroma of fresh meat fills their nostrils. The creaking and cracking of bones echoes as the weight of a three-year-old male lion strains the impala's neck. After a series of twists and bumps, the connection finally gives way, and Insele plummets to the ground, landing atop his brothers.

Meanwhile, the impala's lifeless body collapses on the opposite side of the knob thorn. Dazed, Insele lies prostrate, the impala's head cradled within his paws. Jelwana and Ufudu slip out from beneath him, sprinting forward to indulge in the feast of the impala's body. Insele recovers his wits and savours the minimal meat on the head and neck, then fights his brothers for a bigger slice. Afterwards, they engage in mutual grooming, collapsing into a slumber that carries them through two days. During that time, they hear lions roar. Instinctively, they set their course eastward.

CHAPTER 12

The three lions exit the false-thorn thicket and return to the grassland and basalt plains, crossing towards the S28 dirt road where they stroll south for a few kilometres, smelling the lions that were active here.

On the road, a tourist car trails them, taking pictures of the youngsters as they pad on, indifferent. They come to a clearing with a dam known as Mac's pan. Magic quarries and white raisin bushes surround it. The area is flat and open, and they lie under a yellow flowering white raisin bush during the day's heat.

Jelwana's head rises with movement to the north, as two large male lions come padding towards them. He gives a short warning growl, and both Ufudu and Insele rise. They burst into the grass down towards a drainage line where water is streaming at paw height due to the summer storms. Helmeted guinea fowl and Swanson spurfowl alarms rise behind them.

The two male lions are on their scent. The youngsters push hard, but the warnings die, the sense of pursuit quells, and they relax. The young male lions are used to being on the run. The arrive at a large green tree called a fever tree in a valley close to the S28. Historically, transport riders in the area thought that this tree was the cause of malaria fever. Of course, malaria is caused by the mosquitoes that breed in the swampy areas where these trees grow. That revelation was only made a few years later, but the name 'fever tree' stuck.

Fever trees are one of the only species of tree on earth whose green bark performs photosynthesis, the process normally only carried out by the chlorophyl in plant leaves. The bark, leaves and roots are used in traditional medicine to treat a variety of ailments and in one of those great ironies of the bush, the bark of the tree was found to be an effective treatment against malaria due to its anti-parasitic properties.

The lions rest at the bottom. Water is nearby in the stream, and they nap and recover from their efforts, watched by the red-billed buffalo weavers that have made a large untidy nest on one of the branches.

While they sleep, a lion watches them, the collared lioness from the Vurhami pride. She is out of sight on the eastern side of the S28 road. Four lionesses and six sub-adult cubs are with her. The other pride lionesses are out on a walkabout and the males are elsewhere on their territorial patrols.

The three resident Gomodwane males are large dark-maned lions – scarred – but their dominance proven. They had recently laid claim to the Vurhami's land, the Shishangeni pride to the east, and the Hippo Pools pride to the west. The three young males are now close to the basalt plains of Crocodile Bridge – one of the most predator-rich parts of Kruger Park. They arrive when the dust of major conflict has just settled the three Gomodwane males had pushed in after their dispersal. Three males in their prime, larger and younger than the incumbent Shishangeni coalition. The Shishangeni had once been four, but wild living and rule had through the years whittled them down to two broken-toothed warriors that held onto this prime real estate. The Gomodwanes arrived in the territory and they lived for a brief period in a synchronised dance with the two remaining male lions of the once mighty Shishangeni lion coalition, posturing, displaying dominance and acting from both sides preventing direct confrontation for a period. The area was charged with a strange atmosphere of heavy expectation as to when and how the showdown would culminate.

Then, as so often happens in tales of war, basic instincts got involved. A lioness in season from the Hippo Pool's pride was the catalyst. She strode into the Gezantombi link road one misty morning with her tail snaking and the Gomodwane males following like puppies. The Shishangeni males smelt out her pheromones and could not let the mating rights slide and the long-awaited conflict took place with the two old battle-tested Shishangeni males charging in. Initially it seemed that the two old-timers' daring assault would succeed. The Gomodwanes gave ground, running heavily with reverberating roars bursting out over the African dawn sky.

It is easy to dismiss a male lion as placid when you observe them doing what they mostly do, lazing around, but when you see and hear them in action, the power they hold is arresting. A running battle began that moved into thick foliage near the S25 tourist road. The noise rose in a crescendo, as they fought out their duel unobserved by humans.

Conservationists like to state that we can see only a minimal percent of the Kruger from the tourist roads. In the unobserved wilderness parts, one of the most photographed lion coalitions in Kruger fought a private battle to the death. The Gomodwane younger cats with superior numbers came out of the thick foliage with blood on their muzzles. Scavengers must have devoured the Shishangeni lions as we have not seen them since that day.

Romantics like to think they have dispersed and are living out a retirement elsewhere, but where do wild lions go these days? To areas with other dominant lions? So when your day is done it is better to go out fighting for yours.

The three mighty Gomodwanes rule today but are victims of their success. Ruling such a vast land, they have to spread themselves thin, making sure that their rule continues. Ufudu, Insele, and Jelwana are fortunate; the males are patrolling elsewhere. A day ago, one of the Gomodwanes was in attendance with the Vurhami pride in this immediate vicinity. He followed the lionesses but heard his brothers calling and departed west towards the Hippo Pools pride territory. Lion can recognise who roars? Science has proven they can. Scientists played the resident male lion's roar to a lioness at her den site, and she just rolled over and slept. Then they played a male lion's roar from another area, and she got up and moved her cubs to a safer place.

A lioness watches the ignorant young males. Her eyes face forward with binocular vision that helps lions judge depth and distance, but this means she cannot see behind her and has a large blind spot. We understand her eye position as humans have similar vision. In fact the original human inhabitants of the Kruger, the Khoisan, whose artwork adorns many a rocky outcrop in Kruger, often feature animals, so they are considered one of the first naturalists to study and record these creatures. The Khoisan state that the lion has an instinctive fear of us as they recognise us as fellow predators due to our eye position.

The lioness startles when a sub-adult pounces on her rump, she hisses a low warning, and the youngster moves away. She gazes back towards the young lions. They are lazing in a ravine near one of her pride's favourite den site areas, but no one needs it currently. In these circumstances, she will not draw attention to the pride by getting into a scrap with these upstarts. She instinctively knows that a few sprained muscles can hinder a hunt although she has a pride to assist which enables lions to push the envelope more than solitary cats. She knows a fool's errand instinctively. These three young males will be dealt with through the appropriate channels – the Gomodwane males – when they find them, if they find them. Or these males will do what young sub-adult males do, move off. They are not yet mature enough for the responsibilities of an adult lion.

If they had shown any threat to the pride, or even tried to introduce themselves, the lionesses would not baulk at getting physical with the young males but discretion is the better part of valour and instinct drives her motives. She turns around and walks west, to the territory's western boundary away from the three intruders.

CHAPTER 13

I nsele, Jelwana and Ufudu laze under the fever tree for two days recovering from the fleeing rush, staying put while they suss out their next move. Lions roar all around them, some in the distance, some closer, but none near enough to prompt action. They can tell if it is a male or female roaring, and how many are roaring, displaying a basic understanding of different quantities. The males seem further to the west, a pride of females to the east, closer. And even though the lionesses seem less of a threat during their recent self-rule, they head south because they can hear no lions calling from that direction.

They stroll along the spruit; the brush is dense, and Natal spurfowl with their orange legs shoot off in alarm. The blue heads of the helmeted guineafowl give the three lions a few frights as they are flushed from the tall guinea grass that frequents this drainage line. In a marula tree, an old carcass of an impala hangs. But it is dry skin and bones, so they stare at it and depart once they've determined it is not a meal.

Crossing over the S28 in the ravine on a low-water concrete bridge, they continue to pad south. The landscape opens. In the distance are trees which look unusual in that they are growing in rows all at the same height. They move towards the tree line and crest a rise. Below is the Crocodile River, flowing towards the sea between them and this tree line. The river is broad, brown, and loud where turbulent rapids flow through smooth water-worn rocks, glinting in the sun. On the other side of the river, they see a fence for the first time. And past that tree line, planted as wind protection for crops, they gaze upon sugarcane. They stare at the reason no lions shout south of them. It is the southern border of the protected area that is the Kruger Park.

They laze under cover of an umbrella thorn and ogle. Tractors move up and down, and people wear overalls and hats. The scene is not what they're used to; the people walking in the open create an instinctive fear. There does not seem to be any food on that side, so they head northwest, padding over the S28 past the powerline two-track road.

Herds of zebra and impala snort and warn. The landscape is too open for the youngsters to stalk in daylight. The herd animals and various herbivores cluster for protection. A herd of giraffes glare in their direction. They come to the H4-2 and traverse into the thick foliage of the Vurhami River. Ebony jackal-berries, sycamore figs and apple-leaf cluster along this perennial river. Most of the year it is a dry river where only elephants dig down in the river sand to access water. In some parts, the bedrock shows and collects surface water for longer. The local lion pride is named after this river.

The three lions penetrate the ravine and gaze towards the left at a man-made dam. They find cool river sand that has evaded the sun and lie down in the shade for a siesta. They're hungry, and the herds of animals on the plains they have just walked flood their minds, spurring them to find food. They get up and pad towards the dam. Hippopotamus snort. A young crocodile slides into the water on their approach. They change direction and cross over the stream whilst it is shallow and then hug the far side of the dam. Vervet monkeys alarm as they do so, impalas snort, and a wildebeest male blows his disdain. Onto a road lookout point they walk, with a commanding view of the water, striding past two tourist cars and continuing west. Russet bushwillows and other trees sprout here, and the lions enter the coverage. They need this advantage for their hunting skills are limited.

Heading southwest through the foliage, they hear the frantic snorting of an impala. Creeping up to the tree line, they peer over the open plains to find the source. One look, and they charge towards the noise. A cheetah, two malar stripes like black tear marks on her face, is throttling a large impala ram. Its legs are kicking frantically with his efforts to flee. Mother cheetah's battle is not over and her focus on the antelope is razor-sharp. The other impalas are staring, rigid and snorting alarm at the cheetah who is snuffing a compatriot. Not one is looking at the lions approaching from behind. All focus is on the hunt. The impala ram is large and struggling, and the female cheetah is using all her strength to control his efforts. Two sub-adult cheetahs join the attack on the impala which causes the rest of the herd to increase their staccato warnings. All focus burns at the three predators. The wildebeest see the approaching lion and raise a warning, but the impala think they see the cheetah.

Insele sees his opportunity and bursts towards one of the distracted impalas. Sinew and muscle strain with the effort, and he hits and tackles the buck with force. He moves to the neck; his throttle bite silences the impala. No battle like the cheetah. The impala burst in different directions as Jelwana breaks towards Insele and grabs a piece of impala.

Amidst the noise and drama, Ufudu charges in towards the cheetah, who looks up, her mouth hanging open and blood on her muzzle. She stares into a charging lion, she chirps a warning that sounds like a bird, and the cheetahs scramble away from their meal. Ufudu seizes the injured impala and kills it immediately.

After a few minutes, the lions have gulped down their first few chunks of meat. Hot, they drag the two carcasses into the greenery and eat under the shade. The cheetahs slink off in the opposite direction with sleek concave stomachs and long rudder-like tails flicking in frustration. The lions gorge; two impalas, for them are a meal of substance, not a feast but a meal.

CHAPTER 14

Saturated with meat and blood, hours later they head to the Vurhami to drink, much to the delight of the tourists that often encamp at the Gezantombi lookout. They walk past a vehicle with no sides and staggered seats. They can hear sounds like chattering birds; they often hear this near these vehicles.

The guide smiles and turns to the guests. 'Guys, they have a kill in the treeline there. We can tell by looking at their mouths – the red stains and matted look on their muzzles is blood. So thirsty work, they're going to come to drink.'

The lions walk towards the water.

'What do you think they killed?'

'Too dense in that treeline, I can't see for sure. But I heard some buzz from people that witnessed it go down, that it is impala.'

'How old do you think they are; they seem young?'

'About three or four. See, the manes lack any colour or real substance. The body size is growing, but not near the over 200 kilograms the big males get to.'

'Where is the rest of the pride?'

'These seem like young males dispersed by the pride. Male lions get to about three years old and then get kicked out. Some studies say they make the decision themselves. But I have seen the adult male lions encouraging this on a few occasions. Not pleasant, but it has a purpose.'

'What purpose would that be? Oh, look he is chasing after him.'

'They are playing, full bellies, so joie de vivre,' the guide says looking through his binoculars. 'Believe the purpose is this... Imagine if those males matured in their pride, consisting of their mothers and aunts. The outcome would be?'

The question is greeted with silence.

'Don't overthink it; not a trick question.'

'Interbreeding?

'Yes. We see this dispersal of males in a few mammal species including the elephant. But elephants live far longer than lions, so their male dispersal occurs in the mid to late teens.'

'How long do elephants live in the wild?'

'Over sixty years.'

'That is like humans; how long do lions live?

'Well, these guys here... Young males are going through a particularly challenging part of their lives. They no longer have the prides' protection. And they are navigating areas where other lions are dominant.'

'Who are the male lions that rule here?'

'Three massive lions rule, and if they were to find these guys, they would not negotiate. Male lions treat other male lions that are not part of the resident pride as a threat to their territory. Some studies show that only one in eight wild male lions will make six years old. Considered to be their prime here in Kruger and when they are ready to try to take over a pride for themselves.'

'One in eight!'

'Look, they are lining up next to each other guys, and they are going to drink; watch how long they lie there and lap it up... Yip, one in eight.'

'Do the lionesses stay with their pride of birth?'

'Yes, but they can split off to form new prides if the numbers burgeon or food is too little for them. But they usually live out their days in the pride of birth. A dominant male lion might live to see past ten years old. In some rare cases, longer. But the females or lionesses will live to about fifteen as they do not have to protect the territory. They're looked after by the males that defeat the previous males. The lionesses are the prize.'

'Okay... But won't the dominant males mate with their daughters?'

'Possible, but this dynamic is well timed. Lions seem to take over at age six in Kruger – variances are observed in other parts of Africa on this. There have been occasions of later and younger here too. We are talking about the accepted averages for here. Then they live to about ten before they start losing condition and cannot keep up with the young upstarts that try to take over. Then they either go off on a nomad's life or perish fighting. Sometimes they last longer, and yes, they mate with their offspring. But the females become sexually mature at about three and a half to four years of age. So usually, new males have taken over by then. Genetic studies in this region have proven that females are related in prides. And the males are unrelated, which is a sound system. And let's assume the males have hung around a little longer and have, during this overlap, mated with daughters. What do the new male lions usually do to all cubs?

'They kill them.'

'Infanticide is common with pride takeovers. New lions will kill the young cubs under ten months as soon as possible. The lioness will defend them furiously, but once the cubs die, she will come into season, and the males who just killed her cubs will be allowed to mate with her.'

'This might prevent interbred babies?'

'Might... So many moving parts in biology and many presumptions get revised. But a study states that the males are compelled to do it to set the lionesses off into breeding cycles again. Why would they protect youngsters that are not theirs?'

'Still seems cruel.'

The guide shrugs. 'Not pleasant to watch infanticide, that is for sure. But these are animals; they do not have a conscience as we do, nor morals. The lions will kill those cubs even if their predecessors only sired one litter. But often, people, including myself, make the mistake of putting human emotions into what the animals are doing. One thing is for sure, though. And that is that we humans have also compounded territorial problems.'

'How so?'

'We've squeezed these animals into protected areas. They cannot range like they once did over the whole of Africa, into Europe and Asia. There is little wilderness left so we will see more territorial drama. But we must also think of the human viewpoint when it comes to wildlife. Often, tourists come from areas where wildlife was wiped out centuries ago so their kids can play safely in their yards. And the people living in these areas pass judgement on others; the others whose children can't play safely outdoors. Or those who work in the fields where they may encounter dangerous animals. Would you be happy with a wild lion around your home and kids?'

The guests shift a bit in their seats.

'Do these young guys here have a chance?'

'Better chance for three of them than one. But still a tough life.'

'This dynamic of the resident lions killing them if they find them seems cruel.'

'There is also a purpose behind the territorial behaviour of these animals. It spreads their footprint. And it causes them to self-regulate. Their territorial nature makes it difficult to over-populate because of this design.'

'Really?'

'Think about our safari this morning? We have seen vast herds of herbivore animals, like zebra, wildebeest, giraffe, and impala. Animals with home ranges might fight for breeding rights, but their numbers grow in far greater numbers than these territorial cats. These are the first lions we have seen. That is why when people go on safari it is the most asked-for animal from guests. And I understand that. The lion is Africa. But it is also because they are sometimes challenging to see as they're spread out and have territories.'

'Shoo… they're still drinking?'

'Thirsty work, this navigating these pride lands. To give you a bit of background of what these youngsters are up against. We had a comparable situation recently. The pride here is the Vurhamis, named after this spruit before you. They had six sub-adult male lions that dispersed recently. They moved west of us and into a private game reserve between Kruger on the southern side of the Crocodile River, called Mjejane. We were optimistic, we had watched these young lions develop around here and saw them get their marching orders. And when they went on to Mjejane, we thought six of them could hold their own. But alas, over a few weeks, those three big boys killed all, bar one, in various skirmishes. And now only one is left, living on borrowed time somewhere.'

'That's hectic.'

'Sometimes we find a pride with one resident male. But that is rare here in this wildlife-rich area. Only male coalitions hold territory.'

The guide picks up his binoculars, scanning the foliage on the other side of the dam.

'And we nature guide get far too involved in these animals' lives, like watching a soap opera.'

The guests chuckle at the lame joke.

'Soap opera might not be the right term, more like the Game of Thrones.'

The guests laugh a bit more at that.

'And these days it's not just us, I get lots of feedback from my social media posts from people all over the world that have vested interests and knowledge of the individual lions… They are coming back, guys. Remember to stay seated, no sudden movements we don't want them to get a fright and run from us but walk straight past. Normal talking is natural; they will have no issues. Take pictures but do not scream or shout. Please keep your body parts inside the game viewer.'

The lions walk past the safari truck, and camera shutters burst amid excited murmurs. The guests are impressed at their close-up view of the magnificent creatures. The guide takes a breath and knows what he has to say. He constantly repeats this to his guests when they see something interesting to get them to appreciate their role in the scheme of things. He has repeated it so many times that it feels flat in his mouth and he is conscious of the fact he has to be enthusiastic.

'This experience has also been possible because you are using your hard-earned money to pay the not-inconsequential conservation fees. As a result, these lions get to roam wild lives. So, give yourselves a pat on the back,' the guide says as he starts his vehicle and drives off.

CHAPTER 15

Insele, Jelwana and Ufudu laze next to the kills for two days. Hyenas are savvy enough to know the scraps are not worth the effort.

They hear lions to the east and the west so they head north again along a two-track road that juts from the lookout point. It's late afternoon, and they stride past the cars at the lookout point in single file and down the two-track road. No one follows them. This management road is used for the bush braai facility, so they have it to themselves.

A large male leopard emerges on the road a hundred metres from them. He looks towards the three cats and bounds off and in a fluid movement, the leopard leaps up a knob thorn. He stands in the fork; the three young lions stride to the bottom of the tree and gaze up. The leopard stares down but does not even bother to hiss or growl. He reads the situation; these three cannot trouble him up here.

The lions lie down under the tree. The leopard walks along a branch and lies down with his legs hanging on either side, balancing seven metres up. The leopard seems far more comfortable on that branch than the lions at the bottom of the knob thorn. He gapes down at his temporary captors with yellow eyes and round black pupils. He also has white markings under his eyes to help reflect the starlight and moonlight at night and has exceptional night vision. Like most mammals, leopards have fewer colour-detecting cones in their eyes than humans, and they probably see fewer colours than we do. His face is broader than the female leopard's but nowhere near as large as an adult male lion. His face has spots, and this leopard has a lopsided pink nose with black in it, and scars from an encounter with something sharp.

His power is in his shoulders. These cats are not as bulky as lions but they can carry large animals up into trees to stash them, climbing with the dead weight of the meal gripped fast in their mouth.

Most of his pelt is a golden orange, but his belly and the underside of his tail is white, seen when he walks holding it curled up. His fur is patterned with round black half-circles that face each other, like two facing c's, or an o broken in the middle, called rosettes. He is colours and spots. If you had to observe him with a white background in a sterile setting you would say that he would be easily seen. But in the bushveld, particularly the thickets where he likes to ambush his prey, he is as clandestine and hidden as can be.

Extremely long whiskers sprout from his muzzle. Biologists believe they can determine vibrations in the surroundings with these and the size of pathways through the brush to enable them to move through a thick area without making a sound. His yellow eyes are encircled in black that looks like eyeliner.

The leopard glares down at the three young lions. He decides he has been patient enough and opens his mouth, baring his canines and wrinkling his nose. His pelt scrunches and bunches around his eyes, but a fire burns in his eyes. The snarl shows his weaponry and his intent to use it, although he emits no sound. The lions pretend they are not affected by this death stare and slumber under the tree. The leopard lies back down on his branch and falls asleep.

The young males wake up later and leer up at the knob thorn. They have tired of their indifferent hostage who has only readjusted himself in the tree for additional comfort. They yawn, stretch, and lope off. The movement is perceived by the imprisoned cat and he glides down the tree and melts into the environment.

The lions head back to the two-track road padding north. They come to the fenced-off area for the bush braai. They sense humans, but no one is home. So, they skirt around it and go into the Vurhami riverbed that bends around the bush braai facility. The cool sand under the shade attracts them, and they fall asleep again. Later they are awakened by people talking at the bush braai. They lift their heads; the voices are above them. Because of the angle of the Vurhami riverbed with water-weathered steep sides, the guests are unaware of them, so they fall back asleep.

During the night, they hear three male lions coming closer, so they head due north. They intersect the H4-2 tar road, which is pleasantly warm, and they stop walking and prostrate themselves on it as the sun rises in the east. Cars pile up until the lions have caused a Kruger traffic jam of twenty vehicles. Two tourist vehicles, double cabs emblazoned with animal bumper stickers and Kruger Facebook group specialisations stickers and two large red faux rhino horns on their grilles are camping out. A few people behind are getting impatient with the anchors, hands are gesticulating, and voices are rising. A SANParks support vehicle that has somewhere to be is marooned at the back.

The young lions are indifferent to the traffic they have caused, as indifferent as the two double cabs. The lions roll and recline on the road. These vehicles have never harmed them, and they stare at the long lenses pointed at them rested on bean bags. The two anchor cars refuse to budge from their prime position. A hooter sounds. People gesticulate and you don't have to be a sign language expert to decipher the gist. The lions have heard this sound before around cars and no danger came, the tar is warm, and the grass on the verge has morning dew on it. They have no intention of moving.

The SANParks vehicle crawls past through the grass on the opposite side of the road. It stops and tries to get the attention of the occupants of the cars, but they ignore him. He shrugs and drives off. Others follow the SANParks car and glare into the two anchor cars, but the occupants do not look back. The sighting eventually opens. Those that want to pass do so on the verge, and others wait in a queue that does not move because two will not. The two double cabs have large lenses pointed towards the sleepy cats. One's engine is idling, which despite all the wildlife paraphernalia stickers is a basic bush etiquette fail, as the noise and smell of the engine drown out the natural sounds and no matter how good the bean bag, if the occupant wants to take sharp pictures a vibrating car is not a platform to achieve that.

The lions sleep and the tourists stare. The anchors move off, other tourists park nearby and watch the three youngsters, take a few pictures, and then continue. A few keep their vehicles idling, and the collective sound and the smells of fossil fuels become too much. The lions go into the grass on the verge to hide and the traffic disperses.

After a few hours, they listen to cars drive past, unaware of their presence. Only a tail flick occasionally betrays their position as they chase the flies. Night-time falls, and they get up and walk along the road again. A car, an open safari vehicle, finds them, and the torchlight washes over them as they walk. The guide gives them space and idles behind. He switches off his engine and rolls down the slope after the three young males. Guests ooh and ahh at the three youngsters and then move past and motor off to new sights and sounds.

Darkness envelops the youngsters as they walk on the road northwards. Easy going, no thorns or foliage, and the road rises from the savannah so they can see further. A spotted hyena follows behind them in the distance on the tar, far more confident in the lions' hunting than the lions themselves.

In the distance, Jelwana notices something and slinks off into the grass. Insele and Ufudu follow, as low as possible, crawling through the grass. Ufudu hears a zebra blast air through its lips, much like a horse. The sweet smell of grass chewed by these hindgut fermenters teases their nostrils. Crunching reaches their ears. Taking down an adult zebra will be a stretch at this age, but Jelwana locks in. Insele sees that he is staring at a young zebra foal beside the mare. They fan out, and Insele takes the middle. Ufudu goes back over the road and uses the leeway of the road to stalk unsighted, slithering along till he is parallel with the zebras. Insele leaves the centre position and moves to the right with Jelwana. They writhe close to the zebra, low, scraping their bellies, the grass parting as they inch closer and closer still. The rustle of the grass moving over their fur may seem loud in their ears but the zebra don't notice.

There are five zebras, three mares and two foals. One of the mares stops eating and looks up. The lions freeze, the zebra gazes and chews on grass, then goes back to eating. The wind is moving south on this night. The lions are now at opposite angles, and the zebra in the middle. Jelwana and Insele slide to within ten metres of the zebra. From a standing start, both launch an explosive charged sprint that streaks, their paws strike and grip and their lithe cat bodies bend and manipulate. The zebras have eyes positioned on the sides of their heads, and they see the movement immediately. At birth, the foals have the same length of leg as their mums and they can sprint.

The zebras instinctively break from the tawny blurs streaking towards them. Bolting across the road, their hard keratin hooves slip on the surface and a mare slips. She slides along the tar as her foal slips too, but maintains her footing. Ufudu has been anticipating a young foal. As it breaks over the road, he leaps with forelegs and claws extended. He snares the foal's rump, and they tumble in a heap as he goes for the neck and snuffs out the foal's life force. The mare skids off the road and tries to rise. Insele and Jelwana tackle her with force, the sound of flesh smashing into flesh, and she goes down, trying to kick, but has no leverage. She tries to bite at the lions, but they wrestle her down with their combined strength, one on the neck and one holding her down like their mothers had done countless times.

The other zebra mill about calling their mournful call. The lions pant. The hyena approaches and starts his hysterical laugh; they take turns chasing him off. As they eat, more hyenas appear and the noise crescendos. They first abandon the foal to the hyena, which appeases the mob. Then the hyenas finish that, break it into pieces, and head in different directions. The lions eat from the backside of the mare, the hyenas eat the far side. This status quo carries on, both these predators eating the same carcass. Eventually the hyena numbers swell till it is about twelve against three and the lions abandon their meal and head off into the night. All they can do is listen to the crunching bones and calls as they walk along the road northwards. A lion roars near and behind, and they pick up the pace. The noise of the hyena has attracted the Vurhami pride. Though they have full bellies, this discomfort is temporary; meeting other lions could be permanent. They trot along, and the sounds of a lion pride and hyena clan having a disagreement lessen; they start to relax.

They are safe for the moment and their bellies are full again. A full-grown lion can eat about forty kilograms in a sitting. And like true teenagers filling out, the young lions like to eat. The jog becomes a walk. The night is quiet besides the fiery-necked nightjar, and the call of the water thick-knee, a small plover-like bird that forages at night. A river depression near the southern S130 and H4-2 junction provides cover. They lie down and slumber, staying in the area for three days until they digest all their zebra and their stomachs dictate that they move again.

They had seen a blue-eyed leopard and its cub in the distance. But they would not chase after it in the midday heat, nor draw attention to themselves. They proceed at night, but now male lions roar from the north, and they hear females as well, not close but near enough to pay attention, cupping ear cones in that direction and listening to who is calling.

They come to the H5 road to the west, the lion roars dictate their move, and they head along the road. They find the Vurhami River, walk the concrete low-water bridge, and continue west. They can smell by the marking on the road that it is a territory boundary. The roads form natural boundaries or territorial channels and the cats use them as scent chemical bulletin boards. The young lions are becoming used to the nervous energy caused by travelling these parts.

A water thick-knee bird takes off before them, and they stare. They groom each other and play and gather themselves and continue, the starlight amplified in their eyes. The night-time is bright for them as they navigate the wilderness. A giraffe glares at them over a knob thorn. It is chewing the cud but stops as the young lions flick their tail and stride down the road. Impala snort alarms, and they amble past, aware they have been observed. Tamboti tree thickets hug the road, and the dark puzzle-like bark seems almost black at night. A greater galago calls out the high-pitched frantic call that gives it the common name bush baby.

The Southern Cross and pointer stars are visible and Orion's Belt illuminates from high. They are close together this night, and the atmosphere makes this appropriate. Tamboti thickets open to a large sodic site, and the lions sprawl in the opening, all facing different directions, lying on top of each other like a collapsed ruck.

They are nervous that night but the lack of drama eventually dissipates the fear.

CHAPTER 16

D awn breaks with the lions napping in various prone poses. A tourist discovers them with paws in the air and the lions peer back at the people staring at them. As the sun rises, they seek shelter next to the motor vehicles. Flies cake their pelt from the zebra kill. They flick their tails and use their forepaws to wipe their faces, as we do after a swim, to rid themselves of the pests. A kid in the tourist car is fascinated by the multitudes of flies, taking off but settling almost immediately when the appendage is still again. The swarm of parasites irritate the lions, but cannot stop the lions from slumbering, spending the entire day in different yoga poses.

The afternoon heat languishes late but slowly starts to dissipate. Insele, Ufudu and Jelwana stretch and yawn, oxygenating the brain for movement. They stand up and walk west along the H5; cars follow as they stride along, and then the cars leave to get out the gate. It is just them and the open road. Dense sickle bush thickets grow next to the road with bright multicoloured pink and yellow Chinese lantern-looking flowers. A hyena whoops its mournful long contact whoop. A pearl-spotted owlet gives its call that sounds like a climax. They huddle close and walk as one.

Daytime finds them on the road. Jelwana's head is up, Ufudu on his back and Insele with his head lying over his forepaws snoozing. Five days after their last meal, they're starting to feel empty. Tourist vehicles find them again, using the shade to their advantage. Cars drive right past a few metres from them, but the lions lie in the shade of the stationary vehicles. Insele goes to a pothole that has some water left in it and drinks until sated.

At midday, they start walking, looking for a meal. Movement in the foliage alerts them. As one, they stop and stiffen and stare with absolute tangible focus, all the muscles and ligaments tense, the cone opening of their ears funnelled towards the movement – listening, smelling, and gazing. Insele breaks left, low to the ground in a crawl. Ufudu stares forward, and Jelwana breaks right, like Zulu King Shaka's bull horn formation. Ufudu writhes towards the movement, each foot fall measured and paced.

A kudu bull with large spiral horns is browsing, its dark tongue wrapping around leaves and pulling them back into his mouth. At the angle he is feeding, his horns sweep back to near his spine. Two white tips on the ends of the horns betray his age. He has fine white stripes breaking the solid outline of his body, an effective camouflage. His body is a rich grey, and he is almost invisible to the human eye and known as the grey ghost. The sound of his chewing betrays him, and his scent fills the lions' nostrils. The large ears of the kudu are constantly moving in different directions trying to discern any potential danger – one faces forwards, and one faces backwards, listening.

The lions move in slow motion through the grass, inching forward. A kudu barks, the sound like a gunshot. One of his compatriots has seen the lions. Immediately alert, the kudu stares toward the alarm rouser. It does not bolt but stands and stares, instinctively knowing that to run could result in an ambush. The alarm rouser stares at Jelwana. The targeted kudu follows the gaze of his brethren. He barks and bounds away a few metres, tail curled up, showing the white under-neath. It stops, turns, and barks again. The kudu is primed to flee; the ambush tainted. Two tourist vehicles enjoyed the whole spectacle. Some occupants were disappointed they did not see a kill, and some were relieved they did not. The young male lions rise sheepish and the kudu herd bark their disdain at the audacity of the lions.

The lions come together and groom each other. They shake it off and walk along the road again, hungry whilst the kudu males stare at them with large dark bright eyes, barking their alarm so all will know danger is near. Tourist cars follow. A leopard tortoise is on the road, drinking water from a pothole. It sees the lions approaching from afar. It turns and makes for the grass at top speed, faster than one would imagine, though not fast enough to escape a lion.

Jelwana beats Ufudu to the tortoise. The leopard tortoise knows the drill. He hides in his shell as the young lions drool, trying to manipulate him and his hard exterior. A lion's jaws can crack it, with patience if not treated like a toy. The lions play with the tortoise more than endanger it. They carry it around in their mouths but drop it, pick it up, slobber on it and try to chew on it. The diameter of the tortoise is too large for their carnassial shearing teeth. The circular curve of the shell makes their pointed canines slide off, the teeth that give them the name carnivore. After frequent swats, chews and slobbers, they drop it for the last time and dismiss it.

The leopard tortoise is the right side up, and he waits for them to depart down the road before he sticks his neck out. He plods into the grass to hide another day with just a few scratch marks on his residence.

CHAPTER 17

S ome distance away, two large male lions have picked up the scent of the youngsters. Padding quietly through the long grass, they are gradually closing in on the unsuspecting intruders, searching as night falls.

The male lion has a circular scar on his muzzle that looks like a smudge. Known as Smudge, he was often found around the Lubyelubye area near Lower Sabie rest camp, with his brother who was called Fudge because of a redder fudge-coloured mane and the matching phonetics. They have moved into the S82 area, pushed by younger upstarts from the Sabie River. Although they are holding onto the S82, they are essentially nomadic again.

As humans, we often imagine that animals experience the world as we do, but a wonderful word called Umwelt describes how animals perceive the world using their unique and acutely sensitive senses, able to detect surface vibrations, smells and sounds too faint for us to detect, and echoes and magnetic fields. Animals are closely attuned to their surroundings which is why they are able to seek each other out in the wilderness.

Smudge stops in his tracks as he cuts the trail, sniffs and whirls the scent into his nostrils. Fudge follows but is soon distracted by some vultures in the distance and pads towards them. Smudge, confident, keeps his head down and his nostrils are full of the young lions' scent as he follows a trail as obvious as following a string on a pathway.

With each step the scent grows stronger in his nostrils and he vibrates in anticipation.

Without warning, the tall yellow thatching grass at the side of the road parts as Smudge torpedoes in with speed, cavernous mouth open and teeth bared. The young males bomb blast apart. Jelwana heads left, and Insele bolts along the road. Ufudu jinks and sidesteps past the storming lion, using his attacker's momentum to evade contact, like Cheslin Kolbe in the SA vs England World Cup rugby final. The male lion locks into Jelwana's stride as the young lion darts for all he's worth. Smudge is gaining on Jelwana as he runs through the brush, tree branches whipping his flanks, and his breathing becoming heavier. Sand sprays up from his strides as paws scoop against the soil, and lactic acid builds in his muscles.

The large male lion's mane streams behind him with each stride, blowing in the wind. He emits a growl that sounds like a cold diesel engine starting and the fearsome sound spurs Jelwana to new heights as he flees, his scrubby tiny mane wispy in the air.

Smudge has far more weight on Jelwana, but the youngster's leg-to-weight ratio is better and he starts to create a gap, gracefully bounding over a small river into the brush. Smudge locks his legs and slides to a stop. His tail whips in frustration, and he lashes out his front right paw at nothing. He turns in different directions looking for the young upstarts. A few years ago, from the position he ambushed them, he would never have missed. Now here he is hearing paws kicking up dust as they flee. Smudge opens his mouth wide and lets out a cavernous roar. The sound comes from deep inside his belly and crashes over the bush. It is answered faintly in the distance by Fudge. The thunderous sound enters the young lions' ears and they sprint as far as they can for as long as possible.

Much later, Insele and Ufudu find each other, but Jelwana is alone. Insele and Ufudu do not contact call; they do not want to give away their position.

They instinctively know now is a time to be silent as they move with haste through the brush in retreat. After hours they start low contact calls, trying to hear from Jelwana. The bush is silent in lion response. They meander together with their heads hanging; tired and hungry, they continue, too frightened to stop. They head south, the night air feels heavy, and they collapse in a heap, hyperventilating, lying on each other.

Night becomes day, and in the morning, with their heads up in different directions they contact call and contact call, but Jelwana fails to answer. They spend the day grooming but there is no play. Day turns to night, and they recline under an African sausage tree and contact call occasionally. One of the large fruits that give this tree its name falls and lands next to Insele. He jumps and growls at it in fear.

When day dawns they realise they must move to try to find some food. Above them, in the African sky they see vultures circling and coming down. Usually, they would avoid this as it could be a lion pride on a kill, but their hunger forces them boldly towards the scene. They move cautiously, stop, listen, and smell, satelliting towards the descending vultures. They come closer still, noticing that the trees are not full of waiting vultures. Instinctively they realise these are not lions on a kill. If it were, the vultures would wait their turn.

Approaching with caution, the lions stare out at a dead rhino, its horn hacked off, the smell of humans. Hyenas and vultures worry the carcass. A white-backed vulture is on top of the carcass, its wings spread wide. A long foghorn-like call emanates from it. White vulture dung streaks the carcass and down feathers garnish it.

Hyenas are inside the rhino; faces and spotted bodies streaked red with blood and flesh. Spotted hyenas consume the meat around the loins and anal region first, then open the abdominal cavity and pull out the soft organs. The rhino's stomach lies to the side.

The two lions storm in. Hyenas and vultures scatter. The vultures take off and land in the dead trees nearby. The hyenas gather, chatter, laugh and rally. The lions lunge at them; they give way. The two lions commandeer an opening that the hyenas created. The hyenas forget the class war and eat the carcass on the other side. The lions eat their fill, and as their bellies burgeon they glance from the carcass to see if any other lions appear. Their mouths hang open wide, and they hyperventilate.

Eventually, Insele goes to the shade for a snooze. Ufudu finds more space in himself to eat more. Then he sprawls in the shade of a knob thorn next to his brother. The vultures flood the kill and share with the hyenas. Hyenas are now also spreading out in the shade around the carcass. Occasionally, they cast an eye towards the young lions. All that stirs are their distended bellies as they breathe and their tails flick away the omnipresent flies.

Often, a new hyena appears from the brush, and the noise increases. The hyenas sniff each other's genitals in an unusual greeting ceremony. The hyena females are larger and dominant, but are hard to identify as their genitals look like the males, with elongated clitorises that look like a penis, even with the bulbous tip. They can even get a pseudo-erection. They have no vaginal opening, but have intercourse and give birth through their clitoris. In the early years of biology, hyenas were incorrectly thought to be hermaphrodites.

The dominant nature of the female hyenas makes them even fiercer than the males. When a pack of hyenas kills prey on the plains of Africa, the females eat first, followed by their offspring, and then the males.

The lions stare at the greeting spectacle but are far too full to dictate terms on the carcass. They spend the night slumbering and in the cool early dawn they eat again.

CHAPTER 18

A few kilometres away, Jelwana crouches in the thickets, alone and hungry. He had seen the descending vultures the day before but his instinct warned him that other predators would too, so he ignored his hunger and stayed hidden.

This morning the sky is no longer full of vultures, and he stares in the direction they descended but does not walk towards it. He moves in the opposite direction, lies down, and contact calls a few times, listening for a response. None comes. He tries again, hopeful, but his call goes unanswered into the bush.

Insele and Ufudu's heads are in the rhino carcass, eating to their heart's content. A thirst is growing. Heading off from the carcass in search of a drink, they find a shallow depression with water. They slink beside each other lapping the water with their tongues, their eyes roving from side to side as they quench their thirst. After they drink, they head back to the carcass where the trees are full of vultures.

Three lionesses surround the carcass with hyenas spread all around them. The lionesses see Insele and Ufudu; they flatten their bodies, snarl, and growl. Tails flick and whip. Insele and Ufudu spot no males but turn tail and run south with their bellies large and swinging, running until they reach the S25 sand road. Finding the broad flowing Crocodile River, they retreat up the sand road again and lie under a marula tree. The shade and full bellies placate them into a deep slumber for most of the day.

A tourist stops and takes pictures of the two young lions sleeping. Now and then, they open their eyes sleepily and look up, and a host of camera shutters and oohs and aahs go off into the African sky. Night-time descends, and still they sleep.

Jelwana is drawn to the direction of where the vultures descended. It has been three days but perhaps he can pick up some scraps. He heads to the site and sees the carcass illuminated in the moonlight. Thick grey skin pulled back, exposed ribs. Bits and pieces all over where the hyena have spread themselves. He strides out into the clearing, but the growls that assault his hearing turn him, and he flees south.

The three lionesses get up and watch but there's no need to pursue him and chase him away from the meal. As he runs, his stomach empty and his life alone, his nose picks up a familiar scent. His pace gets quicker as the faint scent becomes stronger. He follows it, and walks over the S25 road with his nostrils close to the ground sniffing and smelling. He goes up and down, a few times losing the smell. In his frustration, he lets out a contact call and his brothers, lying flat under a marula tree, put their heads up in unison. Both stand and come to greet him; the contact calling crescendo grows ever louder. They rub their muzzles together, play, groom, and lick, then crumple in a heap under the marula.

Now and then, Jelwana looks over at his siblings and vocalises softly. Although he is hungry, he falls asleep next to them, the three lions lying against each other.

CHAPTER 19

The following day brings about two full lions and one hungry one. The Crocodile River streams past and the lions explore the bank. Sycamore figs line the riverbank, and the lions walk through the shade provided by the large trees.

The game is plentiful, drawn to the area because of the water and vegetation near the river. Jelwana is keen to keep moving; the full-bellied others are less inclined to. Jelwana does not let his brothers out of sight. He does not want to repeat the last few nights.

A large herd of impala spreads out over the rolling hills before them. Hundreds of buck, many eyes, ears, and nostrils, the impalas' two-tone countershading colours of rust red and tawny as far as the eye can see. This herd is mainly ewes and young sub-adult rams from the previous breeding season with the occasional large ram dotted about. Dark metatarsal glands above the rear hooves stand prominent; it has been suggested that the scent released from this gland may act as a chemical cue for other herd members to follow during a chase. When fleeing from danger, the tail is raised to expose the rump, which is marked with distinctive black and white stripes. These 'follow me' signs on the impala rump and tail look like an M tattooed on their bums and act as a highly visible marker for other individuals to follow during the explosive scattering of the herd that occurs when they are ambushed. Ewes are making grunting bleating sounds and the young impala lambs are near the middle of the herd in a large creche, a few weeks old but with long legs and the ability to sprint.

The wind is in the lions' favour. Jelwana goes into stalk mode. The food before him drives away his insecurities about losing his brothers again. Insele and Ufudu lie down under an apple-leaf and watch. They do not join in the hunt.

Jelwana crawls into the wind, his nostrils full of the scent of impala, inching his way through the grass quietly. When an impala looks in his direction, he freezes. He creeps closer and closer, his ears flat and his tail low.

Two nyala bull antelope are measuring each other's status. They are holding their heads high and walking parallel to each other. The hairs on the back of their body stand erect, yellow legs that look like crazy socks making slow, high steps. Their tails are curled back, white hair displayed on the underside.

Jelwana shifts his attention to these two distracted nyala bulls. One nyala lowers his head with its long spiral horns and moves it from side to side. Jelwana adjusts closer, moving with more intensity because of the distracted nature of the nyala. The bull with the lowered head wags his tail. The bulls are of comparable size, and no submission is shown; the theatrics re-peat. Jelwana slinks within five metres of the two antelope. The nyalas lock their horns and start pushing each other. The noise of the horns striking is Jelwana's cue. He bounds in, tackling the unaware nyala. The three of them fall in a heap; one nyala has Jelwana latched on to it. The other rolls free and leaps away into the brush, the victor through crookery.

The impala herd starts snorting, hundreds at once, like an AK47 dispersing rounds in a spray. Jelwana bites into the back of the nyala as horns thrash about. He rolls the bull and swipes for the head with his paws; his blow strikes home and the antelope is dazed. Readjusting his grip, he goes for the neck and suffocates the antelope with a powerful crushing bite.

Insele and Ufudu might be full of rhino meat, but they still come to make a nuisance of themselves around the meal. The impalas move off, and a hyena appears, drawn by the impala snorting. A male leopard they do not see watches from the cover and slinks off once he establishes he is outnumbered. The hyena ogles, not calling or laughing. Jelwana swipes at his greedy brothers for their efforts. Blood is spilt at the kill, but not only from the nyala; lion blood also seeps into the ground.

Jelwana gorges; Insele and Ufudu fill themselves up further. All three then enjoy a grooming session repairing the havoc caused during the vigorous feed. For two days, they recline close to the nyala, gazing over the river, watching people in cars and on foot from Marloth Park. Some lucky walkers had seen the takedown of the nyala. Crowds have been gathering with binoculars, cooler boxes and camping chairs, comfortable under the shade of the trees on the opposite side of the Crocodile River.

What should be alarming for the unaware Jelwana, Insele, and Ufudu is that there is another crowd in Marloth, a few kilometres to the east. They are watching three large lions known as the Gomodwane coalition on territorial patrol along the river. One has a split scar on his nose from a previous battle, and some call him Split-Nose. Another is large and muscular for a lion; his name is Tank. The other is Scar, as he has a large scar on his face from the takeover from the Shishangeni lions. All are in their prime and known as the Gomodwane male lion coalition.

Adorned with dark black manes rimmed with rust red, they walk with the confidence of ownership, coming to drink at the Crocodile River. They walk past the elephant breeding herds, avoiding the elephant cows that trumpet and encircle their youngsters as they stride by – for good reason, for the lions have eaten young elephant before. They merely gaze in the elephants' direction, navigating with confidence, scent marking their domain, lifting tails and leaving their royal stamp.

The midday sun rises and they find an apple-leaf tree to slumber under, scanning the horizon on occasion as the compulsion arises. The birds shout that they have survived the day and as the sun disappears and night falls, the three large Gomodwane males groom, lick and rub each other, cementing bonds that have stood trials and tribulations.

They contact call and stretch, yawn and then rise with the darkness, padding west towards three contented, unsuspecting young lions.

CHAPTER 20

The young lions listen to the melodic night calls that seem to promise peace. Then a scent jars their nostrils; the scent of three male lions. A crested francolin calls an alarm, betraying the lions' presence. They cannot see them, but they're close.

The young lions glance around anxiously. They move from the kill to the west along the river, walking and checking behind them all the time, not knowing how close their enemies are and hoping not to run into an ambush. The night is dark, and the river noise floods their ears; they head down to the river-bank, and onto the sand bank, turning around, frantic, looking over towards the tree line, where the scent and the francolin's alarm came from. The open ground here will reveal if they are being pursued.

They move west but keep looking back. Ufudu sees the coalition first and calls a short warning as three male lions break out of the foliage and sprint onto the riverbank. Sleek and fast, their chest muscles pump with effort, their strides are smooth and long. Tails extend straight out behind them, mouths are open, slack-jawed, panting with each stride, saliva gushing from these cavities. Scars from previous campaigns criss-cross their bodies and faces. Their eyes are burning with intensity and their gaze is focused on the young lions.

With one glance, the three youngsters know that they cannot outrun these adults. They are in their prime and ready for action. Even at this distance and in the dark, eyes and muzzles betray their intentions. It fills their hearts with dread, and without hesitation they bound into the river. Shallow at first, lapping above their paws, they sprint, water droplets spraying with the effort of each stride.

They hear the Gomodwanes doing the same. The sound of pursuit spurs them on, the river deepens, and they spring through the water, porpoising from the riverbed to gain momentum over the water's drag. Their paws lose traction on the sandy river bed, and they keep their faces above the water with a furious doggy paddle, faces grimacing, contorted with effort and fear as they bob up and down pushed to the east with the current.

The roaring crescendo as the river moves past some rocks masks the sound of their pursuers. They bob over the deep channel, jump run over the mid-depths, and bolt over a sand-bank. Then into another channel that deepens again, forcing them to swim once more.

They finally reach the southern side of the Crocodile River and shake themselves off. Drenched pelts and scraggly manes, their adolescent muscles flex with every movement. Water sprays in every direction but they do not dawdle. Sprinting up the bank, they come face to face with a game-proof fence. Barbed wire with ticking electric wire strands that pulse. They run along the fence until they find an indentation that warthogs have made and they slide under the fence into Marloth Park.

The Gomodwane male lions stand in the ankle-deep water on the northern side of the river, roaring in frustration. The roars are partially drowned out by the rushing river, but the young lions get the memo, 'This is mine, this is mine, this is mine!' The announcement is made for all those with ears.

The wet youngsters take their first few steps outside the protected area of the Kruger National Park. The scent and sounds of humans reach them, but they have no choice but to stay where they are for now.

CHAPTER 21

The familiarity of the bush has gone. Although the lions smell game animals, giraffes, zebra, impala and such, the atmosphere is different. There are houses with humans, some outside cooking meat on a braai. The three young lions pad along the road peering backwards, straining to see if the Gomodwanes are following.

A person stumbles towards them. The lions slink into the bush, hiding between flannel weed and sickle bush. The human, with his limited night vision, is clutching a cell phone, concentrating on the narrow space his cell torch illuminates, unaware that three young curious cats are observing him, their instinctive wisdom telling them that darkness is safety. And there are no apparent resident lions… yet.

They stroll after the pedestrian and his cell phone light, following him on the compacted soil of the road, hearing him breathing and mumbling to himself. He heads towards a house, and the lions break their vigil and pass an open area spotted with umbrella thorn trees.

Then the Gomodwane lions roar in unison from the opposite side of the river, and fear wells up deep inside them as the vocalisations of power crash over them. Their tension dissipates when the sound lessens with the realisation that the adults are not going to cross the river. Tails go up as they jump on each other, playing and expending energy, until they tire and lie down. With bellies full of nyala bull, they lie in the clearing and watch the stars move across the sky.

Before the daytime glow, they navigate into a thick part of the bush and lie in a river course. The river sand is cool, and they relax and digest, hearing cars and people out of sight. They spend two days slack and slumbering on the river sand.

As night falls, they pad into the clearing. An ostrich is in the open, head up, eyes open, but asleep. The lions stalk up to it and Jelwana dispatches it with one swipe. The three lions drag their prey into the river course, and have supper and a snooze. They alternate between wakefulness, play, and sleep, nibbling on the ostrich in between, spending days in this same vicinity in the thickets digesting.

In the dead of night they rise and lurking past the clearing, they find another ostrich sleeping with its head up, but falling a little, and lifting like a yoyo, like we do when tired. The lions stalk, kill it and drag it to their lair. They consume the bird, and large feathers from the world's biggest birds clutter the soil.

The carcasses attract flies, and appendages twitch to remove the swarms. At night they hear the Gomodwanes announcing their rule across the river, but there are no responses from their side of the river. More confident, they stride into the clearing.

Roads criss-cross in more regular grids in Marloth. Impala alarm at them, a wildebeest snorts, and a kudu barks; this has not changed. The lions let the warnings roll over them.

Headlights appear and the lions pad off the road as the lights approach. Gazing from mere metres away, they remain immobile. The driver is lost in conversation with his passenger, gesticulating and speaking loudly. The lions stand like statues in the open without a blade of grass hiding them, watching as they drive past, indifferent.

Striding back to the empty road, they blink as a giant warthog materialises before them, usually not out and about at night. The warthog senses footfalls and identifies a threat. He bolts with urgency, but slips on the dirt. The lions tackle him, pinning him on his back. He flashes his tusks – the bottom tusks razor-sharp from sharpening on the large top tusks when he chews – and bites. Squealing a high-pitched squeal that could wake the dead.

At a home nearby the lights illuminate the veranda, the door opens.

'Be careful, liefie!' a female voice of warning shrieks.

'Don't worry. I have my torch,' a voice counters.

The rotund stomach comes through the door before the skinny legs. Boxer shorts and flip flops and confidence. Liefie shines his powerful torch towards the noise, but the beam of light shines short. Sound travels on cool still nights. The scene is further away than it sounds.

He has a decision to make, he steps into his garden, and jumps vertically as he stands on his garden hose, thinking it a reptile.

Air-karate chops fly and incoherent sounds. Comprehending his faux pas, he chuckles.

'What's that?' his wife calls from the home.

'Nothing lovey.'

Composing himself and taking a few steps backwards he collects his wits with deep breaths. He shines again towards the noise. His light hits trees, and bounces back and his face crumples with the brightness. He rubs his eyes, closes them and reopens and comes forward, his heart beating loudly and his blood pressure zinging in his ears, out of breath, tingling with adrenaline and fear.

The large warthog squeals as the lions battle to throttle his thick neck. Warthog legs kick the air, and blood trickles. Footfalls approach, astonishing the lions. They freeze, as they see a light levitating closer; they blink and then hear a high-pitched scream as the householder's eyes focus. Spinning and screaming with the grace of a sumo athlete, he drops his torch and runs.

The unattended torch beam showcases insects flitting in the dark. All three lions grunt a warning and abandon the warthog who resurrects himself from the brink of death and bolts into the night, protesting his horror. The householder's howls and warthog shrieks amalgamate into one other-worldly Cacofonix-like vocalisation. The warthog's tail sticks straight up in the air as he motors away with a sore throat and healthy new respect for staying in burrows at night. The lions' ears follow the progress of his frantic retreat with diminishing squeals. The three lions grunt again and lope away from the scene, growling and hissing at each other, a close meal lost.

'Sartjiiiiiieeeeeeeee, it's flippen lions!'

'*Liefie*… How drunk are you?'

CHAPTER 22

The lions explore. Following the roads, plenty of game animals reside here. But the warthog has forewarned the animals, and they are wise to them. The resident animals not as used to predators as those living in Kruger, but they are still hardwired with instinctive wisdom. They don't need to be taught about danger; they feel it.

The sun brightens to the east as the faithful golden orb rises above the Lebombo hills. Three people stroll to work towards a building site. They spot the lions and freeze. The lions stare but move off the road into the foliage, hearing excited laughing and yelling, their appearance causing floods of dopamine after the adrenaline.

A black-backed jackal calls its high-pitched wail in the distance. A hyena answers with a long whoop call. The lions discover another fence, finding a culvert where water has eroded a channel. They glide under the barrier into a thin island of indigenous riverine bush, coming out into the sun on the other side. The fields before them are acres of prepared sugar cane farms broken up with natural foliage on the next adjacent watercourse. Retreating into the island of shade, the cats sleep until midday, when they hear people approaching. They raise their heads towards the voices.

'They went out here, see the tracks. In the early hours of the morning.'

They stare, silent and stationary.

'Onto the farms. Let the predator chat group know they have left Marloth for now, but for the residents to be vigilant.'

The sounds lessen, but machines work and people toil in the fields. None come into the thick watercourses. A drizzle of rain falls, and the weather is cool for summer. When night falls they explore the sugar cane. Bushveld rain frogs emit their high-pitched call, in thanks for the rain. The lions hear movement in the sugar cane, but it is dense, and whatever is moving does so unseen.

They pad along the sugarcane maintenance roads, returning to their island of foliage by the watercourse to slumber during the day. When night comes, they navigate to the fence, flattening their bodies under it and entering Marloth towards the game animals they smell on the plains, too attractive to ignore.

Padding along streets and over a tar road, they stop in the shadows as a car nears. The lions wait for headlights to pass, then slink along the tar road, enjoying the warm asphalt, lying down and rolling, playing together. Another car's headlights approach. Apprehensive with unfamiliarity, they traipse into the tree line, wandering through people's yards at night, sniffing, smelling household paraphernalia.

The young lions hear the rubbery lips of a zebra expelling air. The sweet smell of zebra fills their nostrils. Making out movement, they keep their heads down and crouch low to the ground, stalking, inching closer. What they see as their eyes adjust to the lights streaming from the house perplexes them. A woman with bare feet, wearing a satin nightie, stands on a veranda, a bowl clutched in her hands. Zebra line against the railings, staring at the hand that feeds them with the same intensity they stare at a lion. Another human appears. The sight shocks the lions into a lull, a lull that is tested and tempted by their hunger. Jelwana inches a few steps forward.

The boyfriend has his phone out and is photographing his girlfriend. The zebras are nipping and biting each other with impatience, milling around to get their food from behind the railing. The lions watch, their muscles twitching. The zebras munch and now and then, one of their hooves stamps the ground, and they snort and expel air like horses.

'Video me now, babe,' the woman demands, pouting at the camera as she takes a handful of the game feed pellets. She flattens her hand and feeds the zebra, and as it hoovers up the feed with big twitching lips, the woman squeals and smoulders at the camera again.

'Lovely babe,' the Insta-boyfriend replies.

'Let me see?' she asks. 'A bit lower.'

The man crouches down and films. The woman flicks her hair and repeats the feeding process. The zebras are focused on the food.

'A little lower, babe.'

The boyfriend lies on the tiled floor of the veranda.

'No babe, this angle, the lighting comes from high, too many shadows… But I like the view up these legs,' he says and chuckles.

'Babe!' she says, flirtatiously, bends over, whips her nightie up, and flashes him. The light showcases cellulite, he focuses on the good. She lithely stretches back up and then goes back into business.

He films again. A zebra at the back is not getting fed and is agitated, and it pushes and wheezes and whines itself towards the railing. The front row are not delighted and start fighting by biting the mare on its neck. The mare pushes into the melee and gets fed from the hand and then in response turns parallel, whines a high-pitched whine, farts and kicks out, the hoof blow echoing through the night sky. The receiving zebra stands unaffected but Insta-boyfriend almost drops his phone with alarm.

'Watch out, babe! These are wild animals.'

The lions observe this with a mix of fear and intrigue.

The pouting and posing continues.

'My followers are going to love this stuff,' she says, flicking her hair and whipping out her own phone to video the zebra's face, who flares its nostrils wide and snorts, jerking away from the glittery object zooming in towards it.

One of the young suckling zebra foals is jostled by the group and canters away from the veranda, stops, and peers into the darkness beyond the light. The lions' hunger overwhelms them, and they streak towards the veranda, the artificial light bouncing off their tawny coats. The foal backtracks, but too late. The lions rise on their hind legs and leap, collapsing onto the zebra foal in unison.

The zebras panic, neigh and rear up against the barrier. Pandemonium ensues. In the ruck and flying hooves, the Instagram model and film crew drop their cell phones in panic, and fall to the floor in fear, fortunate to evade the zebra scrum. Wooden balustrades crack and shatter with the weight. The mares gather, turn, and gallop past the lions, the ground shaking with the power of their hooves. The mother mare charges, kicking at the lions, and the people screaming, the wood shattering, and the zebra mare's bravery startle the lions. Releasing the foal, they streak back into the shadows. The foal tries to rise onto its hooves, and the mare charges at the lions again.

The Instagram model crawls along the broken barrier. She is in front of her boyfriend, and her nightie hikes up, exposing her, but he notices nothing; he only sees the front door. He gathers himself and flees; she does too. They reach the open single door simultaneously, hitting each other's shoulders and the doorway, collapsing into the house, groaning and writhing with pain.

Adrenaline gets them up, slamming the door, and straining to see what is happening in the yard. The zebras and the foal are gone. The lions too. Everything seems quiet, but the compulsion to go out and collect their phones lying on the veranda amongst parts of shattered balustrade is quelled. A debate of chivalry and equal rights erupts.

Jelwana, Insele and Ufudu argue too at each other and their missed opportunity. So close yet so far. They pad into the darkness, but the zebras have caused widespread panic. They saunter and as the bush settles, the lions find themselves back at the clearing, where another ostrich is snoozing. The lions kill it and eat it there, steadily decimating the flightless birds of Marloth.

CHAPTER 23

T he lions head back to the farm and the island of foliage. There are weird distractions in Marloth, but there seem to be no lions or hyenas, and plenty of food, so it is a workable scenario for them. They sleep in their refuge under a large fever tree for days before they feel hungry again. Once again they hear the voices of people, but the sound dies down at the fence line.

The next time when they come underneath the wire of the fence line in the darkness flashes like lightning occur. Each time one of the lions comes through the flash triggers. It's bit disconcerting but there's not the large noise that usually accompanies lightning. It's more like the noise they hear from the cameras when cars stop for them in the Kruger National Park. Jogging a little faster into the greenery and houses of Marloth, they search for a meal, heading towards the ostriches, but no ostrich this time.

In the dim night-time light, they see a tower of giraffes. What intrigues them is not the adults but the youngster. Almost two metres of baby giraffe with his dry umbilical cord protruding from his belly, wobbling with tentative steps. The lions melt out of the shadows in a jog. The mother giraffe startles and runs but the youngster stares transfixed. The mum turns back and charges past junior for the lions. The young giraffe follows its mother as she strikes out at the lions with her front legs. But the lions sidestep her and hit the giraffe calf. It topples, and two pin it down as Jelwana goes for the throat.

The mother circles back and rushes for the lions. Ufudu growls and charges her and keeps her engaged. She lopes and kicks with her back legs as Ufudu chases her along the plains, till he breaks off the chase and lopes back towards the calf.

The young giraffe succumbs. The mom stares helplessly from above as the lions start eating. A car with a spotlight drives along a parallel road and shines on the scene. The sounds of the kill cause the predator WhatsApp chat to buzz. A stream of cars heads to the sighting, and soon the lions are encircled with torches. Ravenous, they eat despite the distractions. The cars switch off their engines and listen to the crunching and chewing. The grunts and groans as Jelwana, Insele and Ufudu devour their kill.

Dawn breaks, and the lions are on their backs displaying swollen bellies. They are lying on the plains near Seekoei Drive, which hug the fence line of Marloth Park and Kruger. The Crocodile River is not the only thing that runs here. The route is popular with joggers and walkers in the morning, observing animals whilst getting some exercise. This morning a runner with tall colourful socks squeezed into Hoka Speed-goat trail running shoes is out. He wears tight neon shorts stretched over his bulging quads and a luminous vest, his hair held out of his eyes by a logo-emblazoned hairband. This neon image jogs along the fence line, puffing the fresh morning air. His muscles are filling with lactic acid and his body screams for a break.

He sees the cars to the right encircled around something and decides to investigate. A nearby giraffe stares down. This is a chance for him to catch his breath, maybe take a selfie with the giraffe. He takes out his AirPods playing Snoop Dogg, and strolls towards the action. The lions hear something moving towards them and look up in unison. All ten cars flash lights. People scream, and the runner halts in his tracks, confused. He spots the three lions, muzzles covered in blood. No longer confused, he knows he should stand still. He has read books. He has watched shows. He has imagined this scenario hundreds of times as he runs the river road from his home most days.

He recently deleted the predator warning chat because people post nonsense, about neighbours talking too loudly, breathing too much, running generators and all trivial stuff as if this place was run by the Gestapo. This town is meant for vacation use, no permanent residents allowed just holiday homes, but that is not being enforced, thank goodness, because he stays here permanently. His neighbours are all older folks with too much time on their hands, joining committees and groups and talking a lot but changing nothing.

None of that has got to do with predator warnings. The chat group does not seem so tedious now though. His brain is firing rapidly down all sorts of trails, avoiding the lions in his vision. He has never experienced such procrastination of thought. No life flashing before his eyes, but rate payers' associations and retirees that he actually could not give two hoots about. Others confronting such danger talk about a singular focus, this is not his experience. His grey matter grasps for normality. What will the honorary rangers think about me being chewed by Panthera Leo? A group WhatsApp going out… 'We told you so, but no, you don't listen. You choose to walk and run, knowing Kruger is adjacent, now we have to destroy these lions, we told you so.' Maybe in capitals and definitely with too many exclamation marks.

This thought that he will validate these types angers him and drags his mind back to the present. It seems like an eternity he has been standing with his mouth open and solving Marloth's issues but it has been a few brief seconds.

Nothing can prepare you for the flight-or-fight reaction of encountering a big cat on foot. Only experience can, and this is not often experienced in the modern world.

His brain screams STAND STILL whilst it fires these random thoughts of distraction. His legs don't get the memo and despite his brain knowing what should be done, his legs have a mind of their own and he turns and runs like Usain Bolt. He sprints, knees high and arms pumping, joints and sinews popping and groaning at the speed. He bounds along the fence towards his home with his watch shouting at him to slow down as his heart rate soars. His retreat run is motivated first by terror, but the last half motivated by shame as he had run in front of the WhatsApp brigade and he is sure there is already cell phone video footage being zinged around the innerweb with his inglorious retreat in HD. Mortifying.

CHAPTER 24

Ufudu, Insele and Jelwana gaze at the colourful creature bolting from them. Their bellies full, they roll over and could not be bothered. People are screaming, some are laughing, more engines move near, and it gets crowded. The youngsters rise, yawn, and stretch. They walk towards the shrubs. Cars follow them, but can't drive through the green belts, so the lions stride direct, and no one dares to follow them on foot. Soon no cars are near them as they move along Marloth roads in the daylight. Again, they meet staff walking the road towards them. The staff stop and watch them stroll into the bush. They duck through their fence; the flashes of light are not as bright in the daytime.

In their refuge, lazing about in various states of lethargy with bellies full of giraffe, they groom and play. They vegetate for three nights and then head into the sugar cane fields on the fourth. They follow the maintenance roads, sensing movement in the cane. The movement increases, and a bush pig breaks out. They chase after it, the bush pig sees them a fraction too late, and they fall upon it.

There are no distractions this time, and the lions eat their prey at their leisure. They laze around the carcass in the middle of the sugar cane field. No vehicles disturb them. No person walks past, and they pass the day eating and sleeping next to the kill on an access road in the sugarcane field.

Clouds drift overhead and a tawny eagle finds them, he glides above but moves on. They hear the Gomodwane lions roaring and announcing on the opposite side of the river. They listen, and Jelwana even contact calls, not a roar, and Ufudu and Insele stare at him like he is crazy. The youngsters are beginning to fill out, bodies thickening and hardening. Since they left their natal pride, the constant stream of protein by hook and crook has been key.

They stride back to their foliage line that has become their lair, as dawn rises. They spend a few days playing and much of the time sleeping. Some studies say twenty out of twenty-four hours are spent inert. As night falls, they slink under the fence into Marloth. Confident; the sounds from houses and the people they see have not harmed them. They play, rumble on the roads under darkness, pushing deeper into the conservancy and coming across the southern game fence. At the fence, strolling along it, looking for a hole, Ufudu spots a warthog under a house's wooden deck. Entering the deck from all angles they grab the sleeping warthog and pull it out. Human smells are present but faint; no lights are on. The sounds they make emanate into the African night with no response. The lions gorge on warthog in peace and spend the next two days under the deck in the shade.

In the late afternoon, they hear a car approaching the house as the sun nears the horizon. It drives along a two-track dirt road, and they can hear its engine growing louder as it navigates the challenges of bumps, rocks and holes. The car pulls up under the shade port and stops, the engine switches off and tings as it cools down. The lions survey from under the deck as doors open, and a man gets out and stretches; his wife alights from the other side.

'Oh, wow, right on the Lionspruit fence,' she says.

He opens the rear door and removes a suitcase; she opens the boot and gets a cooler box. The people carry it towards the stairs that lead up to the deck and go to the door, unbeknown to them, within metres of three wild lions.

'What is that dreadful smell?'

'Don't look at me.'

The lions wait for darkness. They listen to the couple going about life, confident they are hidden. And when night sets, they squeeze out and walk. No other lions have been sensed in the time here. They mark, scent, and brush against foliage; they want to claim this area. They don't roar though; they don't want to attract attention to their new-found lion vacuum. They can't defend it. They spend the night checking under decks for warthogs, finding one juvenile asleep, dragging it out and killing it. Lights blaze, and whispers commiserate. Some cars and torches arrive, but the lions depart in the morning like they have learnt to do, striding to the fence line that hugs the Crocodile River, spray marking as they go.

Two aged walkers come towards them on the path. The man with a red cap, the lady with silver hair. Looking up, and finding three lions walking towards them. They freeze, and shout at the lions who stare at the noisy humans and move into the vegetation. The two walkers watch with rapt attention as the cats circle past them.

They return to their refuge, and camp for a few days in the thick bush, happy with their little existence and the lack of other lions, grooming and growing their bonds even closer.

In the evening they walk through the tall sugar cane fields and onto the rich red soil of the roads. Black irrigation pipes snake the road, and they explore and play. The cool night air lulls them into lying on the road. Night becomes day, and they laze on the dirt road in the middle of the sugar cane field. They sleep all day until a pick-up truck drives the road in the late afternoon and stops next to them.

'Stations here on the farm, Sector C... Got those three young male lions Marloth rangers were talking about the other day. Over.'

'Copy. Over.'

'They are lying in the road, flat cats. Over.'

'You know what to do. We must keep the workers safe. Over.'

He sighs and reverses the pick-up Toyota twenty metres. His wheels squeal with dust on the brake pads. The lions gape towards the noisy retreating vehicle. He opens the car door and steps out. Steel-capped leather slip-on safety boots and khaki socks, short khaki pants and a two-tone shirt, multiple tools and a holster attached to his belt. The lions are now very interested and stare intently at the man standing before them.

He takes his parabellum handgun from his side holster and points the gun. He triple checks that there is no one behind the lions, cocks the weapon and aims. He takes a deep breath, lets some of it out, then holds his breath and steadies his arm. He squeezes the trigger. The gun kicks in his hand, and a bullet cleaves through the air and into the ground to the left of the lions, where he aimed the shot.

The explosive sound and the whistle of the bullet resurrect the lions, and they race from the noise, bounding as fast as they can away from the din. The farm hand aims again at a point close to the fleeing lions and fires, taking care not to be too close. The sound encourages them to sprint even faster.

The man gets into his pick-up and drives after them, speaking into his radio.

'Lions are being encouraged to leave the area. Over.'

'Lekker, over.'

'Have lost the visual of lions, last seen hightailing west. Over.'

'Copy that. Will let staff know to be wary in that sector for the next few days. Over and out.'

CHAPTER 25

T he lions bolt into their band of foliage with ringing ears and hide under the fever tree. They are confused and hyperventilating from the effort of the sprint.

Night comes, and they feel more confident in the dark, the nervous energy dissipates and calms, and they eventually fall into a deep sleep, close together, touching each other for reassurance.

Dawn reaches them in the thickets, and a blue-headed lizard stares down from the fever tree. A grey-headed bush shrike gives his spooky cry from the canopy above them – a mournful call that gives him the nickname of the ghost bird. Night falls with them heading into Marloth again where they hunt and sleep under the deck of an empty house.

The following day as they head towards the Crocodile River fence they spot a cyclist. She is wearing spandex pants with geometric shapes that accentuate her figure, a cycling helmet and clip-in cycling shoes. Her leg movements are powerful and practiced as she peddles a bicycle that cost the equivalent of a small car, and the speed and shape she presents on the bike enthrals the lions, who lope after her.

She is staring ahead, focusing on the trail next to the fence and she is oblivious to the charging lions. If she senses eyes on her, she assumes it is some lewd man looking at her bum protruding into the air as she cycles standing up on the pedals. Well, the eyes are male and focused on her posterior, but not in the way she imagines.

The lions chase after her. Her husband follows far behind with his head down, breathing heavily, deep in his own meditative thoughts. The couple had arrived from Johannesburg late yesterday after a serious board meeting about some crisis somewhere, that might make him lose a lot of money.

Music blasts into his ears as he glances up to find three lions bounding after his wife. His brain cannot compute for a few milliseconds. He opens his mouth wide and screams a blood-curdling scream that even he can hear over the words of the song.

She whips her head around at the exclamation. She chose not to wear earphones after the guesthouse owner warned them about predator reports. Though heard many times when they visited Marloth, they'd never had any issues. People were too dramatic, they thought, so both had decided they needed exercise. After all, being eaten by a lion was something that happened to other people, people who sleep in huts on rural plots, not educated, successful couples like themselves, who need exercise to decompress after their demanding important vocations.

She sees what is chasing her, but her brain is numb. Base instincts kick in … No research paper written can help her. She is so distracted by the three young male lions bounding after her she forgets to steer, and rides into the game fence. The barbs of the fence slash and gash whatever they touch, including her geometrically enhanced bottom, and she bounces off the fence in a heap on the ground.

The lions are intrigued by this turn of events, but now she's prone on the floor, squirming, but no longer moving at speed on the bicycle. Their parents never taught them how to hunt these human creatures who provoke a deep-seated fear, a fear that is slowly being eroded with each encounter the lions have with humans. But this fear compels them to stare and not rush in closer. It may have been different at night.

All movement now is generated by the husband, who cycles towards them, screaming and pumping his legs on the bicycle. The lions break away in different directions and trot into the bush, leaving behind the crying and sobs and harsh words.

A hippopotamus shouts his snort from the Crocodile River. A fish eagle throws his head back and calls. The lions head for their thickets to sleep under a fever tree.

At night, they head south from their lair in the river course, slinking under the fence and striding out onto the verge of the road. This is unlike any tarred highway they have ever encountered. The tar roads where they existed have been a maximum of fifty kilometres per hour speed zones, in protected areas and conservancies. This road is set at sixty kilometres per hour. A slow speed. But it is tar, rural and in Africa. Importantly, it has very few potholes. This road is ignored by the traffic cops who prefer to monitor the Mozambique heavy traffic of the N4 main highway. So the local drivers treat the speed limit as a hundred kilometres per hour.

The noise the car makes as it approaches is like a jet. As the lights near, Jelwana stands transfixed and illuminated in the middle of the road. His brothers come and stand next to him, moving their heads side to side, trying to glean the origin of the sound. The car has its brights on, and the spotlights shine on the three tawny cats in the middle of the road, the golden light highlighting their natural colours.

Brakes squeal, and burnt rubber reaches their nostrils as the car slides to a stop just metres in front of them. The lions see it is a car. Nothing new but the sounds and smells worry them so they turn around and jog towards their thickets, lying under their fever tree for the rest of the night with a new fear unlocked.

In the morning a helicopter hovers. The lions in the thickets laze as the aircraft flies its grid pattern. It is a yellow Robinson R44, and it is searching. The lions have watched SANParks Airbus Squirrels flying about since young, so they are indifferent. It comes and goes the entire day but they sleep into the night, only stirring the following day when they play, groom, and chase insects in the thicket. It's cool and lush, and they feel safe in its innards.

At night they head back into Marloth, onto quiet roads as they search for any wildlife. They look under decks and search for warthog. Finding nothing, the lions head for a swimming pool; they have developed a penchant for clean pool water. A group of people are sitting around a fire. The flames dance into the night, and they approach the edge of the light, watching as people laugh and giggle and socialise around the fire, before slinking into the darkness.

They come across a kudu herd, but the cows are too alert and bark and run away. The barking causes the impala to snort and a bushbuck to bark, so the lions push on further to where the animals will not know they are out and about. The sound of alarms dissipates as they melt into the darkness, searching for movement.

A person walks towards them in the dark. He is moving sideways, forwards, and backwards. The drunkard has been at a local drinking hall and has had his keys confiscated by the bartender. He's upset at this injustice and is walking home. The lions stare.

'Hello…' he slurs a greeting towards them.

They stare back. The drunk walks on, stumbling, his eyes focus, and he rubs them again, but when his vision clears, he sees nothing but the bush. He shakes his head and mumbles.

'Brandy… makes me seeeee things.'

The lions are alert, now walking through an area with several houses. An illegally-smuggled-in pet Yorkshire terrier is lying on its owner's patio. It sees the lions and bolts into the house, barking mad.

'Cupcake… What did you see?' A large lady in a dress strides onto the stoep, and spots the three lions in the light.

'Jacobus! Lions!' she shouts and bolts inside like Cupcake.

Jacobus hurries to the window, but is too late. They're moving on, from house to house, looking for a meal. A spotted genet slinks away from them and runs up a sweet thorn tree, staring with his large eyes as the lions stride past.

The lions hear hooves and see a dazzle of zebra in front of them. They don't need to stalk; they simply rush in. Zebras scatter. Jelwana lashes out with a paw, and his claws latch into the shadowy stripes of a youngster, who crumples under the weight, and they snuff it, ignoring its mother's protests nearby. Feasting in the dark, they eat as much as they can that night.

As the dawn starts showing, they move, knowing things get crowded in the daylight with humans. Walking towards the Crocodile River, they stare across it to where they once came from. The river slides past, and they settle in their favourite haunt, bellies full of zebra and muzzles full of blood.

They are getting used to not fleeing from the dominant male lions. Humans are clumsy in their efforts compared to a two-hundred-kilogram jealous male lion, with sharp claws and the agility of a cat, who could smell out their presence with regularity when they were in the Kruger Park. The new status quo is less stressful, with no hyenas and no drama. The weird fast machines on the road to the north are more familiar now. The lions are becoming creatures of habit.

They digest the zebra foal as a helicopter buzzes around the area again.

CHAPTER 26

J elwana, Insele and Ufudu stride into the sugar cane one afternoon, their fear of loud noises has dissipated. Night falls with them padding kilometres east, past farm homesteads with ticking electric fences and large dogs that bark at them in the darkness. Compulsions move them north over an empty highway and under a game fence into a large block of natural bush. Moving through it, they sense wildlife but not at the levels of Marloth.

They sleep during the heat of the following day, rise in the afternoon and find a dam where they crouch at the water's edge and drink their fill. The man who owns the hunting farm is in his Toyota Landcruiser, busy on his cell phone as it is one of the only parts of the farm that has signal. He almost drops his phone as the three young lions come to drink and ends his call without explanation. His 30-06 Springfield rifle is lying next to him in the cab, he looks at it with ice blue eyes and picks it up. The lions lie next to each other and lap up water, ignoring the car.

The farmer has seen lions on his land before, often dispersed youngsters, sometimes lionesses, even lionesses with cubs, he has even organised a few hunts of lions on this farm in the past. He opens his rifle's bolt and checks the chamber. Satisfied, he closes the bolt in a manner so practiced he does not need to think about it. His mind wanders to the hunts on this block, where he's releases handsome dark-maned lions bought after being bred, petted and posed with many a tourist, the tourists facilitating the breeding costs. Then he buys them from the breeders from a photo catalogue, organises the permits and the large lions in their prime are carted here and released in this bushveld block.

The poor creatures are so used to cages, that each lion paces along the fence; a wire fence is all they know from their years of captivity. The breeders warned him to inspect for any warthog burrows or culverts or else the lions would find them, go under and pace on the other side of the barrier. So he would shoot an antelope and place it in the middle of the block to lure the lions to the centre of the block in the hope of a meal.

A client that pays a small fortune for a 'canned' hunt does not want to shoot the animal next to a fence; that doesn't look good on the video they will invariably make. He calls them clients because they are certainly not hunters. A foreigner with money and limited time that wants to shoot a lion, will come from his luxury accommodation, disembark from the vehicle, and then follow the professional hunter on foot towards the lion – a lion so used to people that he would sometimes start strolling towards the humans that have nurtured him all his life.

The client then takes aim at the huge, dark-maned lion – fat, because it has never patrolled a day in its life – through an expensive scope over a high-powered rifle and because of their excitement at shooting such an impressive thing, or because they just can't see very well, the client will squeeze off a horrible round, invariably a gut shot. The professional hunter will already be aiming and shoots the kill shot a millisecond later.

It's a practice he personally finds repugnant, but it's legal and profitable if you dot your i's and cross your t's and keep it off social media. The dollar is strong enough to get a pat on the back and well done when the euthanasia is over.

The farmer is under no illusions, he has hunted wild lions before in wilderness areas, tracking for days and bleeding on thickets, sometimes not seeing sign of the quarry. Trudging through areas no tourist would go to photograph anything, scraggly dry bush on hunting blocks far removed from the glitz and plush lodges, these hunting blocks are the only reason the lions exist there.

And he has been charged by lions and shot swiftly from the hip at animals coming fast for him, if he had missed he would be dead and that is not what he organises on his farm. It's a charade, but humans have wants and needs. He then makes even more money from the hustle. The lion bones are sold to Asia. No client wants the bones, just the picture of them next to the dead animal and the skin for a trophy to be displayed at home, so it is very profitable, and in a roundabout way this saturates the demand for wild lion bones.

Wild lions are not poached like the rhinos because there is a legal trade in the lion bones. He likes to focus on that outcome in a debate, although he knows that is a stretch, but he is practiced in rationalising his thoughts, compartmentalising his emotions, just as the tourists who cuddle cubs or walk with lions at these 'centres' compartmentalise theirs. He knows that if you approach a lion cub on foot and the mother is not actively charging you and you are being spat at and told off, it is not natural.

The last time he organised a canned lion hunt on this farm he vowed he would not join the next. He finds it hard pretending to respect a client who would classify that as a decent hunt, while knowing it was a manipulated scenario, facilitated to appease man's search for excitement.

A lion hunt from a catalogue and I'm part of the process, thinks the farmer, shaking his head in disappointment, as he puts his Swarovski scope onto the young lions and studies their scraggly manes. He has shot a few lions in his day. If he had fancy game like sable or roan or the variants of antelope that cost a small fortune on this farm, he would not hesitate to put these guys down, but he does not have any expensive hunting stock on his block, too close to Kruger, too close to predators. He also has no lion bone export permits as he has no lion hunts organised. But he does not want them hanging around eating a kudu so he steps his fit strong legs out of the Landcruiser, and with his arms milling around and the rifle in his hand, he sprints down the dam wall, yelling loudly.

The lions bolt at the crazy sight, the farmer drops to a knee and lets a few rounds boom out to encourage the retreat, laughing at the excitement. Ufudu, Insele, and Jelwana sprint back through the fields and over the road, narrowly avoiding a coal truck sneaking the alternative way to the Lebombo border.

CHAPTER 27

T he lions make their way to their safe spot in the riverine ravine, firm in their understanding that they are safer in the wildlife-rich area of Marloth. They spend a few days inert, resting and lazy, and recovering and slink back into Marloth one moonless night.

The roads are quiet and they pad along, smelling and scenting, finding only their own scent marks. All lining up next to each other, they drink from a swimming pool on a deck. The lapping in the dark goes unheard, and they sate their thirst and walk to the road, flicking their tails and scanning the area. A banded rubber frog lets out a high-pitched melodic call, a trill that lasts about three seconds. It keeps these calls going as they move about in the darkness, keeping vigilant, using sight, sound and scent to detect any prey.

The sound of a distressed buffalo calf fills the night air. A hint of blood hits their nostrils and they move into the ostrich clearing. The lions can hear a calf, but they can't see a calf. In the middle of the clearing lies a zebra carcass with its belly open and innards to the side. Two bakkies are parked to the left of the zebra carcass, with lights off.

The lions move forward cautiously, and stop every few strides, to scan, smell and search for any danger. The metallic scent of blood fills their nostrils and lures them closer. They surround the carcass and settle down to eat. The zebra is chained to a pole. No clashing between them; there is enough to go around. The night air fills with the sound of tearing flesh and chewing, with a few groans.

A red-light spotlight comes on. Jelwana, Ufudu and Insele don't flinch. A pneumatic noise of air expelling, and Jelwana feels a sharp pinch on his rear. It burns, and he snarls and takes a retaliatory swipe at Insele, thinking he is the culprit, before settling and feeding again.

Now Insele feels a pinch after a loud pneumatic noise; he growls and jumps. He tries to reach the point of pain with his mouth, but too settles down shortly and continues eating.

Ufudu sees this, stands, stares at his brothers, and relaxes only when his brothers go back to feeding. He growls at them, and then the sound comes from the car again, and Ufudu is the last to feel the pinch. He snarls and swipes at Insele, Insele growls back and forepaws fly in anger, but after a while, they all eat again.

The sedating drug administrated by the veterinarian needs only minutes to take effect. The lions are immobilised in the order they were darted. First, Jelwana, then Insele and finally, Ufudu – all asleep, dead to the world.

The small team gets out of the vehicles and ensures that none of the lions is in a position which could result in injury. The vet checks their mouths to make sure no foreign objects or regurgitation can choke the lions. Even though it is still dark, he wets their tongues and secures a covering over their eyes. Experience has taught him that when dealing with a lion that wakes unexpectedly, it is better to have their eyes covered. They work fast. The vet scans the cats' vital signs – their respiration rate, pulse rate, blood pressure and temperature, taking measurements, collecting blood samples, and conducting body assessments. They determine the cats' ages to be over three years old.

'These boys are needed here,' the vet says to a fresh-faced, wide-eyed pimply student shadowing the process. 'Look at the vegetation here compared to there.' He moves his spotlight towards the fence, highlighting the lush grass of Kruger creeping right up to the fence line, and then the starkness on the Marloth side.

'Why is it so different?' he says, as he motions for his assistants to bring the stretchers.

'Umm… overgrazing, overutilisation of the resources.'

'Yes, but why would these fellas help?'

'Umm… they keep herbivore numbers down.'

A stretcher is brought, and they slide Jelwana onto it.

'Check the size of his paws!' the student announces.

'He's going to be a big boy. Indeed, they help prevent overpopulation, but they do more than that. Their presence alone discourages herbivore concentrations. It also encourages herbivore movement, which also prevents vegetation overutilisation. They also do my job and the one you have just started studying; they take care of injured, sick, and weak animals.

But I also understand why these householders can't have them walking around their homes.'

'Why don't they cull the herbivore animals here?'

'Some are against it, there's even a moratorium to prohibit it. It's hard to cull when you know the zebra and warthog by name, and they visit your home daily. This area is not truly a natural area. Homeowners feed the game pellets with the nutrients the animals need. But this is also a problem.'

'Why do they feed the animals? Most protected areas don't.'

'True, but look around. This strange, protected area is really a housing estate with wild animals. It's been here since the '70s and has this established wildlife-housing dynamic, with this foliage. If the householders did not feed the animals in Marloth they would starve. But there another knock-on effect besides ethics. What you think it is, young man?'

'They burgeon to numbers that are unsustainable because of the feed. The natural vegetation is over-utilised because of the increasing numbers, and the feed compounds the problem.'

'Bingo… Yoh, clever nè? The animals would starve or move off if this was an open natural area, because there would be no food nearby, which would lead to…?'

'The vegetation being left alone. The landscape would recover with succession plants coming into play.'

'The lion's job done without the lion, except it would take much longer. So you see, their purpose is far greater than people realise. Also, in conservation, can you recall the buzzword?'

'Umbrella species.'

They drag Insele onto a stretcher; the vet checks his response.

'Can you explain it to me in simple terms?'

'People want to see the lion on safari, so they pay to see it and protected areas are maintained for these charismatic species. The less-exciting creatures, say a frog or fish or insect also have a purpose in the ecosystem, of course, but no one will pay to see them except those with niche interests. So the uncharismatic animals enjoy the protected area too. And the buzz of the lion protects all the others. Like an umbrella.'

'Exactly. Could not have said it better myself. The problem is there is so little space left for the wilderness that we have these buffer zones, and areas where we see too much activity, like here. That's when human–wildlife conflict takes place. There are only so many Kruger National Parks left in the world. Vast ecosystems that are large enough to be like Noah's ark as bio reservoirs.'

Ufudu is dragged onto a stretcher and the veterinarian and his assistants carry the lions to the back of the bakkie. They load all three, and the vet stands on the back monitoring the lions during the brief trip. They drive in convoy through Marloth Park where the honorary rangers are at the gate waiting for them.

CHAPTER 28

The sedated lions are escorted into Lionspruit Nature Reserve. The bakkies drive to the area known as the vulture restaurant and the team offload the slumbering trio, habitually rolling them onto the opposite side they were transported in.

The veterinarian monitors their vitals. He is satisfied with their condition, so he administers the antidote into the large veins in the lions' rear legs and leaves the student to observe the lions from the vehicle while they recover from the anaesthetic, ensuring no hyenas or scavengers can hassle them while they are vulnerable.

Their new home is Lionspruit Conservancy, a game reserve located in the conservancy area of Marloth Park and covers an area of 1500 hectares. It was created so that dangerous game could be kept away from the houses and had three lions at one stage, two neutered lionesses and a male. These lions had passed on due to old age some time ago and the area had been devoid of lions ever since. Until now, when the decision was made to introduce these three young lions after much lobbying and politicking by the residents of Marloth.

A woman had broken her collarbone after riding into the fence and her husband had threatened to sue Marloth municipality. A video went viral after a jogger sprinted away from three lazy cats. Residents were complaining that their favourite warthog had become a snack. Something had to give. Mpumalanga Tourism & Parks Agency were mobilised into action.

The lions finally wake from their deep sleep, still groggy. They walk a few metres to a marula tree and pass out again. They are aware of people but are exhausted, only waking again under cover of darkness. A zebra carcass is near, and they eat and return to their usual horizontal position. Hearing the Gomodwane males roar, they peer out into the darkness, but the sound comes from far away, and they slumber.

During the day, they move to shade and laze about. At night, they stir and check out their new environment. It's bushveld, exactly like Marloth but with no houses and more grass. They pad about in the dark, lethargic and find a spot under the stars to sleep off the remnants of the medicines.

In the heat of the following day, mouths open and panting, they set off, striding past dams. They gaze upon giraffes, kudu, impala, warthog, and common duiker. Two large white rhinos, with their horns removed, smell the air and move their ears like satellite dishes in different directions as they pad past. Red-billed oxpeckers blurt their alarm call as the lions stare at the large mammals. African buffalos glare at them from the shade.

The roads are few and far between here, and the scent of people is not as varied nor rich as Marloth. They don't smell any lions, so they rub themselves against bushes and spray mark their presence. They don't roar yet. The day's heat ends, and they laze on the open field, watching the different birds. White-backed vultures pick at the zebra carcass, and hooded vultures use their long slender beaks to access the meat scraps from carcass crevices that the bigger scavengers miss. The large lappet-faced vulture with its distinctive bare, red head with skin folds on the neck is a threatened species and one bird has a yellow tag for research. All these scavengers are essential though they won't win beauty competitions.

In the evening they walk until they find the fence – about two and a half metres tall with a ticking electric pulse. The lions walk along till they find an indentation under the soil that a warthog has dug and they slip underneath the wires back on Marloth Park roads, hunting. The night air is fresh. They walk and scent mark, past the ostrich opening and see no ostrich. Past their capture sight, but no zebra leftovers. Moving stealthily through the houses in the still of the night. They go to their ravine, slink into their thickets, where they stay for a few days, lying on their backs and playing, grooming in the comfort and familiarity of their space.

But hunger eventually draws them out and as night falls, they walk the Marloth roads. The bush baby screams its baby-like call, and the Crocodile River can be heard splashing and roaring along. A thunderstorm lights up the sky, anvil-shaped cumulonimbus clouds pulsating with near-constant flashes of electricity. Rolling thunder crashes down over the Marloth area. The wind whips tree branches, and the lions' senses and acute hearing are overloaded with stimuli, reminded of their recent encounter at the sugar cane field and hunting farm.

The wind rustles and then dies as the heavens open in a deluge. They sprint for cover but become disorientated and head to an area they have not explored, running as the thunder crashes round them, bombarded by the cacophony of sound.

Eventually they come to the Lionspruit fence. As the night sky illuminates with a flash, they find a channel some animal has dug to get under. They crawl into Lionspruit finding a red bushwillow tree and collapse under it as the rain falls, coats matted and manes clumped together. Streams of water develop along pathways, drainage lines and sand bottoms rush with water.

They don't sleep as the spectacle of the thunderstorm crashes over them, their heads are up, and they pant. Rain pelts down, and then as if a switch was flipped, the rain stops. The three boys stand up and shake themselves, water flying in all directions, and droplets of rain from one lion landing on another. After a few minutes they pad in the dark along pathways still streaming with rain.

They come to the vulture feeding station where the birds are in trees roosting for the night. There is a fresh kudu carcass where a black-backed jackal feasting. The lions rush in and remove his inclinations to stay. They lie around and gorge on kudu.

The next morning they lie under the marula tree as ranger from Marloth Park arrives. He dumps another carcass off in the plains; the lions watch this with intrigue. Humans have never fed them in their lives before. In the Marloth Conservancy, if an animal is sick or injured, treatment is impossible; it's put down to stop the animal's suffering and brought to the vulture restaurant. Now also a restaurant for the lions.

The thickets with fever trees are starting to fade from their memories.

CHAPTER 29

Insele, Ufudu and Jelwana settle in their new territory. But being male lions, they still walk at night. And sometimes during the day, they explore Lionspruit. They don't see many people here, just the pick-up that occasionally comes in the morning to drop a carcass. Sometimes the pick-up does not come for a few weeks. Then the lions have to get off their bums and do their own hunting. They run after a buffalo, but when things get serious, they leave him alone. They have success with another giraffe calf, and have developed a habit of hunting wildebeest.

They hear the Gomodwane males calling, and sometimes the lionesses from the Hippo Pools pride. When they hear that, they stop and listen, especially to the lionesses. They may go weeks without hearing a lion's roar. They have begun to irritate the white rhino, stalking and racing after the huge animals. They have made one or two forays into Marloth, but they are starting to enjoy the space of Lionspruit, and have marked all along the boundary fences.

Their bodies are filling out, with the free meals at the vulture restaurant and the successful hunts when no carcass is forthcoming. Their manes lengthen and start to darken.

Two rainy seasons pass, and the males are now approaching six years of age. The locals call them the Lionspruit coalition and they have grown to love and observe the big lions, now in their prime, that roam Lionspruit. People enjoy trying to spot them, which can be difficult if a carcass is not at the vulture restaurant. Finding three lions in 1500 hectares of bushveld is problematic. But they look so regal that many tourists go searching – driving the dirt track route in pick-ups or even low sedans in the hope of finding the Lionspruit coalition.

Lately, the night sky is filled with the roars of Jelwana, Ufudu and Insele, in unison and competition with the Gomodwane males to the north. The Gomodwanes stop and listen when they hear the lions to the south. In the north, the Gomodwanes shout ownership; the Lionspruit male lions shout in the south. Marloth is in the middle of these audio wars. The Gomodwanes come to this side of their territory, marking and roaring. The Lionspruit lions look, smell and cock their ears to the north.

Trouble is brewing.

CHAPTER 30

Summer becomes winter, and the grass turns khaki. Spike thorn trees emit their meaty odours. The days shorten, and the impala are deep into their rutting season, snorting and tussling horns. The three male lions of the Lionspruit coalition use this period to their advantage. The impala rams are so distracted with the rutting that their normal vigilance slips and the lions eat impala to their heart's content.

This boost of protein and the regular free meals increase their muscles and overall health. And with this growth and maturity, their compulsions to find a pride grow stronger.

Staring to the north on one cool evening under the stars, the three Lionspruit lions walk to the boundary fence, find a warthog's hole and slip under the electric wires. Two strands of long dark mane hair remain on the wire. Sauntering through the residents' houses, they don't play anymore; they keep their heads held high, sniff, smell, and mark, and claim the area as their own.

They stroll past a pool and, for old times' sake, halt and drink. A light goes on. A Marloth resident peers out her window. Three dark-maned lions with bodies of 220 kilograms stare at her with amber eyes. They don't stop drinking until they're done and then rise and stride with purpose into the bushveld green belts heading north. Stopping at the ostrich clearing, they roar in unison. Three giant male lions, all facing north, roar.

House lights turn on at the sound. But all go off simultaneously a second later as Eskom switches off the power in loadshedding. A few houses have backup power and other residents come onto the porches with torches.

But the lions are now away from the clearing, walking to the Kruger fence line and padding along the fence to a drainage line. Lowering their heavy bodies down under the fence and walking into Kruger, hearing a Gomodwane lion roaring in the far distance. The Crocodile River is running, but it is winter, the dry season, and it is shallow. Only a channel of fifty metres requires them to swim; the water ripples around their sinewy bodies as their powerful strokes propel them forward.

CHAPTER 31

The three lions near the opposing bank and as front paws make contact, their claws dig deep into the soil, securing their grip. They emerge from the river and shake themselves, water droplets spray. Lying down on the dry river sand bordering the Crocodile River, they gather their bearings, listening for any roar but hearing only the breeze rustling the grass.

It has been over three years since they last saw Scar, Split-Nose, and Tank from the Gomodwane coalition. And it was only a fleeting glance as they fled. They have since heard them bragging in the night sky about the ownership of this land. Now the priority is not to escape, but to claim pride lands. Their noses point them towards the horizon as they rise and walk into the dry grass along a pathway the elephants have engineered to the river, the soil firm and compacted through animals' movement for centuries.

They pad up the path, muscles rippling with each step. The three lions have dewlap folds that extend along the bottom of their belly and swing in the winter air. They lope along the pathway and smell the Gomodwane males. The three take turns spraying, marking, kicking, and moving towards their rivals. Impala snort at them, a waterbuck ogles, and a kudu barks; the lions are not perturbed.

They navigate up onto the S25 road as the sun rises, and a game viewer comes driving towards them. It stops, and the lions move with their mouths open, panting loud enough so the guests can hear it – a deep cavernous sound like an obese person climbing the stairs. The sunrise is behind the game viewer, and yellow light shines on the three impressive males. Six amber eyes in the golden light, the reflective fur under their eyes shockingly white in the sunshine. Scars from quarrels around dinner and their dispersal mark their faces like road maps to maturity. The rusty red around their dark manes is vivid and in stark contrast to the deep black mane that follows, running past the shoulder on their back and far down their belly. With each step, muscles ripple under their tawny pelts. Their mouths hang open, exposing four canines in the front of each mouth, present and sturdy.

They walk past the tourists and the game viewer turns and follows the three big males, the guide excited. He takes pictures and posts them live on Instagram. The S25 is one of the few roads in Kruger that the spotty cell phone signal reaches. The news travels fast that the Lionspruit coalition is in Kruger. It hits the internet algorithm and people from all around the globe give their input from their electronic devices. They know the individuals, follow them, and have opinions on lion coalitions. A host of ones and zeros whizz about the internet regarding the Lionspruit coalition.

Cars file down the road, and the lions seek shade under a purple-pod terminalia tree. They hyperventilate, forcing air over their tongues to cool themselves down, assisted by the shade. They're confident enough to sleep out the heat of the day. Their tails flick to keep the flies caking their flanks at bay. A Cape turtle dove calls its monotonous call. Some say it sounds like 'Work, harder, work, harder, work, harder.' Others, with different priorities hear 'Drink lager, drink lager, drink lager.' Cars come and go to gawk at the lions. The sun descends west, and the golden hues of sunset find the three male lions gazing into the distance with camera shutters going off like AK47 fire.

Night falls, and the paparazzi in the cars leave except for the SANParks sunset drive. He follows for some minutes as the lions head east along the S25 road under darkness. He leaves them, and Ufudu, Jelwana and Insele walk into the night.

Then a roar, followed by a second one, cleaves the air as the Hippo Pool pride announces their territory. The sounds are coming from near the Crocodile River. The three male lions head in that direction, with a measured pace, unhurried. Each step a possibility. Breaking through the riverine bushveld foliage, they stand on the crest of a rise, under the cover of an African sausage tree, rubbernecking down towards the riverbank. The lionesses are spread out in all directions, some with paws pointed towards the night sky.

Tank, the largest lion of the Gomodwane coalition, is on his back, enjoying the residual warmth held in the sand from the day's sunlight. There are no other adult males in attendance. The three lions stare transfixed, observing everything, taking it all in with a heightened sense of awareness. Their muscles twitch under their pelt, but the stare is an intense gaze, with absolute focus. When a lion stares at you, it is tangible.

Five lionesses are here, a few cubs of about five months old and Tank. Tank is the target.

Glancing at each other, the lions come to an understanding; a decision is made. In unison, they sprint down the bank. The footfalls on the sand alert the lionesses, who spin into a crouch and stare. A warning growl erupts, short, deep and sharp, and two lionesses stand and escort the sub-adult cubs away. They hiss and spit, and the cubs follow.

The other lionesses stand, crouch, hiss, and growl a low warning. The Lionspruit coalition has no eyes for the angry lionesses as they run past the prone, snarling females and stride out onto the river bank.

The Gomodwane male rolls and stands tall on his paws and stares. He bares his teeth, exposing yellow broken canines, peering through experienced eyes at the three male lions running towards him. He erupts in a deep growl and bounds forward, rushing straight towards the three younger lions. His body is patterned with scars and marks which tell stories of the many battles and conquests his four-year reign brought. He snarls; huge teeth threaten the three younger males.

The three Lionspruit coalition lions slow to a jog, the Gomodwane male the centre of attention. They meet but don't engage, swiping through the air with paws and extended claws as they circle and measure their foe. Tank spins and swipes and protects his flank. He meets Ufudu, both lions skidding and lashing out with forepaws, razor-sharp claws extended, the noise continuous and loud. Four male lions shouting, gravel-deep growls emanate at different octaves and frequencies.

The watching lionesses growl encouragement, one charges but breaks off when Insele sprints a heavy short burst towards her. Even if you have never heard these sounds before, the savagery assaults your central nervous system. Dry season dust wafts into the air like smoke. Tank connects a paw and claws against Ufudu's flesh, his claws cutting ribbons into Ufudu's nose. The sound is like Velcro tearing apart, as blood sprays like mist into the air.

The blow shocks and stuns Ufudu. Jelwana and Insele move past and bite down on Tank's exposed back. Tank spins to protect his rear. His mouth snarls open; spit flies into the night sky. The coolness of the air mixes with his hot breath, condenses and looks like he is breathing out smoke. Ufudu recovers his wits, and he lunges forward, slashing with his paws on Tank's back as he bites down on Tank's posterior near the spine. The two lionesses with the young cubs run from the scene while the other three lionesses gawk at the battle, growling and crouching low, tails flicking and twisting.

Tank spins and twists towards Ufudu, as Insele and Jelwana bite and slash at his exposed back. Bright red blood streams from faces and flicks onto the river sand with each movement, the metallic smell mixing with the rancid breath of the lions. But they don't whimper or acknowledge the pain, remaining razor focused on Tank.

Their focus is his rear, near his tail on the spine. Tank twists, swipes, growls, and moves, desperate to cover his back. The lions halt with Tank in the middle, breathing heavily, his whole belly heaving with the effort and his back tucked up to limit exposure to his vital organs. He growls and exposes his teeth in a wide-open-mouthed show of his weaponry.

The bush falls silent as the standoff takes place. No night birds call, and the animals are silent after the rising crescendo of the war. A breeze hits the river sand, and the lions pant almost in unison. Blood drips down. Jelwana lies down, and the three attacking lions keep watch in every direction. But they do not look at Tank, the centre of attention. Ufudu's body is angled away from Tank and stiff. Their tails move up and down, and even the lionesses don't stir as time ticks away during the standoff.

Gradually the night sounds return; thick-knee birds chirp, a greater galago calls a shrill piercing call like an infant in distress. Insele staggers stiffly, a few steps away and lies in the sand; Ufudu follows suit, lying in a circle around Tank. Tank's head is down, his hot breath condensing and smoking into the night sky around his cheeks. His hindquarters are tucked low, and he uses his front paws to try to stand. Wobbly, he falls back onto the river sand.

The three lions watch intently as Tank struggles to his feet again. He crawls to the right and stumbles, falling on the sand, sending dust and grains towards Jelwana. This movement sets off the attackers again, and they burst up and move in. Jelwana attacks Tank's face, while Insele and Ufudu bite down on the old lion's rear, grabbing his hind legs and testicles and clamping onto his spine with powerful bites. The noise crescendos again.

The three lionesses follow the scent of the retreating lionesses. One by one, they leave the scene with its foregone conclusion. Sand and blood spray as Tank wrestles and squirms trying to defend himself, but they hold him. The sounds decrease as the three lions release Tank and walk a few metres away, surrounding him. Puncture marks weep from the front and the rear, blood darkening Tank's tan hide. He tries to stand but can't. The three lions watch him, their mouths panting hot mist into the winter sky.

The Milky Way is bright above the battle. The Lionspruit coalition stares out in different directions. Ufudu stands and starts to roar, a loud roar coming from the depths of his belly. The night air mingles with his hot breath, and emerges into the darkness like a rock concert smoke machine. The roar is joined by Jelwana and Insele, and the volume of the Lionspruit coalition booms out for the first time in the Kruger National Park. Not a shout of ownership from outside, not a challenge from Lionspruit or Marloth, but a shout of ownership from inside a pride land.

The sound has been measured, and found equal to the volume of a live rock concert at 114 decibels. This is no contact call, no growl, it's a mighty sound in unison. It starts like a mumble but grows into loud repeats and then tapers into grunts. The lions' entire bodies strain with the effort.

The sound washes over the Hippo Pools area into the Vurhami lions' territory, even into the Shishangeni pride area. We would not hear it at that distance with our human ears, but two adult male lions do. They sit upright and listen, with their ears cupped in the direction of the sound. They have heard this before, but not from where it is emanating now. Without hesitation, Split-Nose and Scar sprint in that direction, eyes focused on the horizon.

CHAPTER 32

Tank's flanks are heaving with the effort it takes him to breathe. His eyes burn with anger. Struggling, he tries to stand again, his muscles vibrate with strain, and he rises, wobbly, from the sand. His body is curved in pain. He is crabbing and stumbling, yet still he comes for Jelwana, his teeth bared, and slashing his claws in sweeping arcs.

Jelwana yields from him, stepping backwards, keeping his face away from the claws. Tank spins and comes for Insele in his crab-like walk, spitting and growling. Insele moves away from the enraged older lion. Tank spins and faces Ufudu and repeats his spirited performance. Ufudu retreats out of reach with a few backwards steps. The three lions stare at the courageous lion in the middle. And they fall on him again, this time not attacking his front but swiping at it from far, causing him to spin and they rush in and bite his exposed back.

This vicious game of tag continues until Tank collapses, exhausted and drained from his wounds. His front legs are stiff, his eyes still burning bright. Three lions grab and pin him and bite and tear. After a few minutes, the natural assumption would be that Tank is dead, yet his tail still lashes in defiance. The three lions hold their bites and struggle against his attempt at defence.

Ten minutes pass with the younger lions gripping, slashing and smothering the prone Tank in a crushing wrestle. His struggles diminish, and the tail movements cease. Finally, there is no more fight in him. Still, the lions grip him tightly. Slowly, the bush sounds return and with the call of a fiery-necked nightjar, the three panting lions release his body.

Without the spark of life, it looks like a shadow of its former self. Walking a few metres from Tank, they stand, hyperventilating, bleeding from various wounds and bites. They flop down near Tank's body, rest and recuperate, and drink water from the Crocodile River.

After their breathing normalises, they rise and follow the lionesses' retreat. The scent is clear, the lionesses have gone up the rocky outcrops near the Hippo Pools lookout. Mountain aloes cling to the rock, their winter flowers full of nectar. The lions move up to the rock where they pause and rest on this vantage point.

The dawn breaks with the three male lions still on the rocks. They roar into the new day. Sunbirds and bees come for the orange flower nectar of the aloes. The lionesses hear the roars of the Lionspruit coalition. They are moving fast, now close to their border with the Vurhami pride. The cubs are tired. They sit down often, but the lionesses spur them on. They can't flee further; they are now moving into the Vurhami territory. Further east and they will be in the core of the Vurhamis and in danger that would not only affect the cubs. The lioness hides the cubs in the block-like branches of a sandpaper raisin bush thicket.

The three male lions stand up from the rocks and stretch and yawn. Setting off over the rocks with noses down, they follow the scent of the pride as clearly as if it were road mapped. Newly confident, they spray mark shrubs and bushes. They come across where a lioness has urinated, and they sniff the urine and flehmen grimace.

They follow the scent like a highway until a growl makes them stop. Out of the thickets, a lioness rushes at blurry speed, spit flies and she slides to a tawny, fury-filled stop. Sand and spit sprays into the males' faces, and they blink and baulk at her fury as she swipes vicious claws toward them. The three male lions cower at the rage of the mother's defence. But they re-gather their composure and approach the lioness, now crouching, tail whipping, with flat ears and exposed canines. The venom in the lioness's eyes leaves them in no doubt she is prepared to inflict grievous harm to protect her brood.

Jelwana takes a blow on his face, rears up and swipes – he hits back but to subdue, his blows not carrying the force he used against Tank, though he will kill if he needs to and the lioness has to submit. The ground shakes with the low growls and the soft oww, oww sounds of the cubs come from under the brush in answer to the noise.

Another lioness flashes out and tries to defend her youngsters. The battle escalates. The males receive as many scratches from the lionesses as they'd received from Tank and the noise is even greater. But whilst the lionesses are busy with Insele and Jelwana, Ufudu bounds into the sandpaper raisin bush thickets, and with bites and swipes, swiftly kills the young cubs.

The lionesses rush in at the sounds, hissing, spitting and growling, vocalising their rage but the fighting ceases and dissipates with the death of the young cubs. The males chase the lionesses in brief bursts in order to subjugate them.

A calm descends after the drama.

The day is overcast with a slight drizzle of winter rain, and the coolness of the air placates the pride. The male lions move from the thickets and sleep in an open space in a deep sleep. The lionesses stare at the males from the thickets. Some groom and lick the dead cubs; others lick their wounds.

The day goes by, and in the late afternoon, most of the cloud has moved off. The area seems fresh and clean in the afternoon sunlight, no more dust hanging in the air because of the drizzle. The three Lionspruit males lie on their bellies, occasionally glancing towards the lionesses, who stare back with venom still blazing.

Then a rustle in the undergrowth causes the three challengers' heads to rise in unison. Split-nose and Scar burst through the bush with savage growls, their manes bouncing with each step, and tails straight out behind them with the speed they sprint. The three Lionspruit males scatter in different directions. Split-nose tracks Jelwana's flight, Scar tracks Insele, and Ufudu circles around, watching. Split-Nose catches Jelwana and trips him with a paw swipe. They both go down in a dust storm of tails, paws and claws. Ufudu rushes to the aid of Jelwana who is on his back with Split-Nose biting his paws. Jelwana is struggling to escape, raking Split-Nose with his rear legs. Ufudu bites down fiercely on Split-Nose's back, and he releases Jelwana and turns on his attacker, who backtracks as the hot breath of his foe washes over his face.

Jelwana is quickly upright and bites down on Split-Nose's exposed back. Split-nose is turning and twisting, trying to protect himself from two opponents. Insele sprints away but then spins around to meet Scar, and they rear up on their back legs to meet and grapple with each other in a deadly triangle. Teeth and claws clash as Insele brings his paw around and twists, using Scar's momentum against him. He wrestles, and smashes Scar to the ground, biting Scar's face. The older lion's rear legs are stiff and slashing the air as he lies trapped on his back, trying to wrangle himself around, but Insele pins him and bites and slashes his face. Tails windmill in their attempts to balance and dust rises, catching the afternoon sun, creating a fiery halo around the fight.

Scar slashes out with front and back paws and gains a few moments of respite as Insele moves back, and Scar squirms loose and gets to his paws. Muscles ripple under their fur as they face each other, circling and slashing, always facing the danger. They circle and circle, pacing and panting, looking for a weak spot.

Scar is bleeding from many wounds. He has been through many scraps and survived them all. The sounds of the other battle reach their ears, but the stakes are too high for them to be distracted. Scar slashes a blow and tries to move in for a bite; Insele jinxes away, and lashes out through the air. The growls and vocalisations crash over the pride lands. An elephant herd nearby trumpets in warning and a Cape turtle dove calls out its call, 'Fight harder, fight harder, Fight harder.'

Close by, Split-Nose is tiring, and the two male lions are taking turns worrying his rear. He slashes and growls and bares his teeth, but as he turns to protect himself, the other lion bites down on his exposed back. Monotonous fighting, but effective. Jelwana bites deep into his back against the bone of his spine, and a loud audible crack carries across the plains. Split-nose's rear slumps, and he is immobile. His front legs can move, but the shock of not being able to operate his hind legs sends him into submission.

The two lions stand over him as he pants, and they gather themselves. Their mouths are open wide, saliva and blood drip onto the dust. Spilt-nose stares into the distance and watches as the lions leave him, rushing to the noise they hear nearby.

Scar and Insele are still swiping at each other, mouths gaping wide, rearing up against each other, trying to gain the advantage. They are in this triangle when Jelwana and Ufudu tackle Scar from the side. The lions roll in the dust, bound onto their paws, and encircle Scar.

Outnumbered, he tries to show submission with his rear down, and his demeanour changes to deference. But the three lions don't heed his response. They pant and relax, not looking at Scar. Instead, they gaze down the Crocodile River towards the sunset, the deep golden colours reflecting in their amber eyes. A waterbuck stares in their direction from an island sandbank, transfixed. Hippos snort, and the sunlight catches the water like glitter. A herd of elephants crosses in the distance.

Scar stares at the ground, blood dripping from his face wounds, they rest as the sun begins to slip behind the horizon. A hyena calls in the distance. A black-backed jackal's out-of-tune call rises. The day is ending.

A soft contact call comes from Split-Nose and the Lionspruit coalition hears and turns. He is crawling with his front legs, his back legs dragging in the soil, pulling himself towards Scar. But the effort is exhausting him. The three healthy male lions watch. A bat hawk flies overhead on the hunt. Scar turns to face Split-Nose and contact calls. Split-Nose crawls a little closer and reciprocates the call.

Ufudu, Insele and Jelwana stand up, yawn and stretch. Then they fall upon Scar, taking turns to increase the damage. The loud sound of bone cracking goes out into the night as his spine is severed. The three lions stand over Scar and roar their ownership. They harass the two crippled lions once or twice more, but the fight is over.

The Lionspruit coalition make their way towards the path where the lionesses ran, nostrils down, gleaning the scent. There is no conscience nor feelings of pride, only compulsions and results. They walk away, leaving the two injured lions breathing, but unable to move.

Split-Nose crawls towards Scar. They lie beside each other, panting, awaiting their fate, a foregone conclusion. The fate they can hear in the distance, as hyenas call their long whooping call. Fate comes closer and closer still until fate is laughing around them. Rushing in, rushing out, until the Gomodwane male lions are no more.

CHAPTER 33

Exhausted from the battle, heaviness overcomes the three victors. They recline at a stagnant muddy waterhole east of the Hippo Pools Road, on the rise next to the S25. Their finding-a-lioness priority has evaporated. Observing the Lebombo mountains from here, all they see is now theirs – their responsibility to patrol, secure, subjugate and dominate. But the first order of business is to sleep – in the stop-start fits of slumber, interspersed with security scans, that are a wild lion's lot.

They arise at dawn and lie side by side, lapping muddy water with their tongues. The reflections in the mirror of the water pool display blood, scratches, and new scars. Blood drips from wounds, makes ripples and dissolves into the murky water. They drink their fill, and spend the day lazing with their paws in the air, grooming each other, rubbing their heads together, and affirming their bond.

Safari cars come and go.

'These are the Lionspruit coalition,' a guide says. The guide sits on his door panel, a strip of leadwood, looking at his guests through his metallic blue sunglasses.

'They come from the Marloth Park reserve. They are pushing into the Gomodwane male lion coalition area. Last night's sunset drive reported hearing an almighty ruckus to our south nearby. And we can see the bateleur eagles and tawny eagles and the vultures descending to the south. So, there might be something dead there, maybe, possibly the Gomodwanes.'

The guests stare at the lions and back at the guide.

'With their scratch marks and fresh wounds, a showdown might have happened last night,' he continues. 'The evidence points to that, and we wait and see if the Gomodwane lions appear. But they were a lot older than these guys; they are their prime, and this is the way.'

'When are they going to do something?' a guest asks.

The guide chuckles, then replies, 'Lions often sleep; we regularly find them having a siesta like this. But they seem to have had a rough night, so that they will rest most of the day. They might move tonight, might not. The cool thing about these lions in this protected area is they do what they want. What their instincts compel them to do, and we get to see them living their wild lives. Which is often this, lying around, excuse the dodgy pun.'

'Can we get some coffee somewhere nearby, please?' a guest asks.

'Sure, there is a place at Crocodile Bridge where we came in. You all happy, can we go?'

The guests nod and look forward to their coffee as the vehicle pulls away.

The lions are sore but restless, and follow the lionesses' scent at night, finding the Hippo Pools pride on a zebra kill. They chase the females off and eat until their bellies are extended. Once full, they waddle away from the carcass and sleep, allowing the lionesses to finish off the zebra.

The male lions shadow the lionesses for another two days and enjoy a further wildebeest meal. Then, hearing the lions of the Vurhami roaring, they decide to introduce themselves, announcing their dominance with roars, marking and spraying over the Gomodwane males' scent. Discovering their predecessors stamps on pathways, trees, and grass, they map their territory. They kick and cover and complete the takeover with every spray.

Two Vurhami lionesses hide at the den site near the S28 drainage line, with their four-month-old cubs. They crouch near a green fever tree, the same tree the three male lions relaxed under when dispersing. Usually, they only use the den sites when the cubs are tiny and helpless, but they have heard the unfamiliar Lionspruit roars. And they no longer hear the Gomodwane's roar.

The lionesses hiding these cubs from danger hear the latest unfamiliar male roars closer still, as Jelwana, Insele and Ufudu approach. They move their cubs from near the fever tree to a site further to the east, no longer in the core of their territory, but on the border with the Shishangeni pride – a buffer zone they use only in emergencies. Hopefully, the Shishangenis will not be traversing this buffer simultaneously. It is as far away as they can run from the danger while still in their territory.

The male lions saunter along the basalt plains near the Croc-odile Bridge camp. Open ground they seem buoyed by the territory. The grass is short, and the red soil shows as the plains game loves to eat the nutritious vegetation found growing in this basalt geology. The males come across the bulk of the Vurhami pride, lazing and sunning themselves in the plains. Bestowed with a GPS tracking collar for research, the lioness named Mariya by a SANParks employee, spots them and bounds towards them. The male lions hesitate, stare, as they try to determine her intentions.

Curiosity compels them, and they jog forward. The lioness flicks her tail and gives them a frosty and indifferent recep-tion. She knows better than to cause conflict. The sounds she has heard and the silence from the Gomodwanes tell her these are the new kings of the Vurhami. Their recent wounds are testimony to that truth. She has been through this before.

The three male lions laze close but apart from the pride. Glaring towards the Lebombo, they glance side-eyed at the lionesses and survey the pride. There are two young sub-adult males, about three years old. Five adult lionesses, and four sub-adult lionesses are present too. One of the young sub-adult males gets up and grooms his mother. Ufudu bursts forward. The lions flee. He hits the young male and they roll in a cloud of dust and sound, the other sub-adult tries to inter-vene and gets a paw swipe for his efforts. This show of strength by Ufudu causes both sub-adult males to show submission by lying on their backs, displaying their bellies and squirming.

The male lions stand erect and stiff and roar into the day. A lioness charges and swipes, emitting a gravelly growl. But she is smacked with a paw that spins her, and she, too, rolls on her back and submits. The male lions mark and kick their legs, standing tall, showing their domination through posture and body language until they are satisfied that there are no illusions about their dominant position.

They lie down and fall asleep. The two lionesses with small cubs catch the roars closer still and lift their noses towards the sounds. Their breathing rate increases.

CHAPTER 34

On the basalt plains of Crocodile Bridge the lionesses hunt as the darkness falls. The two sub-adult male lions follow. The Lionspruit coalition slumber on. The lionesses move across the plains searching with roving eyes for movement. One of them, the lioness Mariya with the collar, climbs a fallen tree and scans the plains before her, spotting a blue wildebeest herd in the distance near the Vurhami River riverine. The person who described them as blue had an over-active imagination. Fanning out, as low as possible to the ground, they stalk closer and closer still…

Then the wildebeest bolt. The lionesses glare back to find three male lions tagging along, walking upright with their tails flicking. The lionesses glance at each other, give the equivalent of a shrug and continue into the still night. The lionesses spot a tower of giraffes in the distance. The male lions still shadow, but a lioness hisses, and Ufudu, Jelwana and Insele grasp the point, finding a knob thorn tree near the H4-2 and lie under it, heading for shade out of habit, as there is only moonlight on the plains.

The lionesses stalk, locked onto a young giraffe. A lapwing emits its alarm, and the giraffes stare towards the sound as the lions bound forward. The giraffes sprint, galloping towards the road with their long stride. An older female is slightly slower than the rest. The giraffe's left front leg touches the ground momentarily before the right, and the rear legs move together in unison at the back. The lions sprint next to her with a matching pace. Approaching the rise of the H4-2 road the hard keratin hooves of the large female giraffe meet tar, and she slides. She slips with the momentum but gathers herself and makes it to the other side of the road without falling, her hooves meeting the earth she's designed to navigate. But she has lost pace, and the lionesses encircle her as the rest of the giraffe herd disappears over the horizon.

Now it is a dance of death, fencing and measuring. The tallest land mammal shoots out a strong kick, a heavy long-legged jab as a lioness nears. The sound of the disagreement attracts the males. A lioness times her jump for directly after a kick, and leaps with her forepaws stretched out and her claws extended. She lands on the rump, bounces, and slides off like an adult off a kid's plastic slide. It looks comical. Another kick flies over the prone lioness's body.

Giraffes can kick with both front and rear legs, providing a 360-degree angle of defence. The giraffe kicks out, one leg at a time, ensuring she has three anchor points for stability. Another lioness springs, claws extended to latch on the back but she also slips off. They revolve around their prey, and the quarry turns, matching the movement, the giraffe not kicking when the lions are not near, conserving energy.

Jelwana sprints in and leaps with his bulk on the rear of the giraffe. He slides off too, and a kick whizzes over his prone body. He rolls and retreats to safety, his tail between his legs. The lions try, but the giraffe is resilient. A young sub-adult male lion bounds in, the giraffe kicks out, and the hoof connects with the young lion's skull dropping him. He is stone dead.

The giraffe outlasts their efforts with well-placed leg jabs, and dancing grace for a large animal. Gravity works against the lion's efforts. They ogle as the giraffe finally strides into the bush. The lioness licks the young sub-adult to rouse it, but eventually gives up and leaves the corpse on the basalt plains.

Jelwana and Insele sniff at the body and roar over it. Ufudu bites it to make sure the young male is dead. The lionesses stare towards the males announcing their presence to all in the area – the same area the lionesses must now try to hunt.

The three male lions follow the pride as they head down to the Vurhami River valley. They pad towards a circular viewpoint of the Vurhami. An elephant has pushed a marula tree over here and the lionesses climb up and peer over their territory, using the vantage point to spot any animals coming to drink. But after the noise from the giraffe attempt and their vocal rulers, no herbivore is relaxed.

A mist appears – a winter dawn mist, often found after clear winter nights, caused by the difference in temperatures during the night. The lions relax on the viewpoint road, waking to tourists materialising out of the mist. Prone tawny bodies line the viewpoint. They would be invisible in the thick mist if they were just a few metres from the road. Cars stop, and shutters click as tourists find lions in their natural habitat.

Ufudu, Insele and Jelwana look towards the horizon, drawn to a territorial patrol. But they are hungry, not having eaten since the Hippo Pools lionesses provided the wildebeest. So they slumber, hoping the Vurhami lionesses will provide a meal.

The mist burns away. The pride gets up at midday, walking towards the powerline junction on the lower S28 road in the late afternoon. Cars shadow them as they pad along indifferently. Halting at the junction, they stare left and right along the powerline's road, checking along the roads to see if they can spot any meals. They don't and continue straight along the S28 through a valley and onto open grasslands above.

A herd of wildebeest is here; the lionesses fan out. The males hang back and do not attempt to hunt; the sub-adult lion also watches. The young male stays clear of the Lionspruit coalition. The fellow young lion he grew up with is now lying on the basalt plains, just a memory. The lionesses stalk to within thirty metres and then sprint after the wildebeest, who bolt in the opposite direction. The collared lioness is waiting in ambush, and bounds out as the wildebeest run by. A wildebeest tries to sidestep the tawny surprise, but she grabs him by the muzzle and is dragged. She applies pressure, and her claws grip deeply into the wildebeest's muzzle. This weight and the wildebeest's momentum trip it; head over heels, it rolls and crashes to the ground as the other lions latch onto the desperate animal. The lioness throttles their prize, and the male lions rush in and commandeer the kill. They fight off the lionesses, who watch from the sidelines as the three males dominate.

Occasionally, a lioness will step towards the kill. The males flatten themselves and lash out, snarls erupt until the lioness takes a few steps back. The male lions gorge until Jelwana and Ufudu leave the carcass. The lionesses descend with Insele still breathing heavily over the carcass, the two ends of his mane below his face are moving together and apart with each heaving breath. He does not protest the lioness's presence because he cannot – he's too full to move.

There's not much left for the sub-adults after the lionesses. Finally, with blood-encrusted faces and distended bellies, the lions scatter to the shade and snooze. They relax near the carcass and groom each other, and then the three male lions get up and walk east, towards the drainage line and along the S28.

CHAPTER 35

The scent of the lioness with the cubs cuts the road. Three males' noses go down to the floor, sniffing at the scent. They move off the road and follow the scent, faint though it is. A few times, they lose the trail but circle until they catch a whiff again and on they continue.

Abruptly, the two lionesses flash out from behind the rocks, open mouths, exposed teeth, and tails whipping, with such fury that Ufudu, Jelwana and Insele run. But they gather their wits and circle and approach the lionesses, who spit and charge to protect their cubs. But the male lions hit out with their paws and bite warning bites. Again, Ufudu sneaks into the brush as his brothers occupy the lionesses, striding out a few moments later, after he has done what he is compelled to do. The three male lions leave the frustrated lionesses, roaring and spray marking as they walk their territory boundaries.

Later, they enter the Shishangeni prides' territory. The lionesses greet them with head nuzzles and no frost. There are no cubs, the youngsters are well over a year old and they are sub-adult lionesses, no young males. They are all weaned, and the lionesses do not need to defend youngsters. So, the Lion-spruit coalition enjoys a warm welcome as benefactors rather than a threat.

The Crocodile River flows into the Nkomati River to the south, with the town of Komatipoort to the west. The Shishangeni pride kill a Cape buffalo on the most remote part of their southern boundary, a small strip of land between the Lebombo mountains and the Crocodile River and people living in houses along Crocodile Road in Komatipoort are out in their gardens watching them with binoculars. The lions stare back across the river past the powerlines. They hear dogs barking and the Mozambique border pulsating both day and night. The three male lions laze for a few days, then head west, marking, roaring and scrape marking. They walk along grasslands, increasing their roaring just before dawn.

Strolling past the Vurhami territory into the Hippo Pool lion territory, they smell for scent and find the lionesses who rub against them and greet them. Ufudu evaluates their urine with a flehmen grimace and determines that the lioness is in season. One lioness rubs her hindquarters against Ufudu's face before jogging away from him, her tail snaking in a playful 'come here' way. Ufudu follows, so do Jelwana and Insele and another lioness breaks away.

The five walk away from the pride with Ufudu and the lionesses in the lead. Moving and stopping on occasion, with Jelwana and Insele following at a distance. Ufudu walks close to the lioness. He stops and checks every time she passes urine, processing it. She rubs against Ufudu's flank, then presents her hindquarters and raises her tail. Ufudu approaches; she turns and spits and swipes her paw, and he stares back, confused by the mixed signals. The lioness writhes on the floor. Jelwana approaches, and Ufudu growls at him; Jelwana comes forward regardless. Ufudu charges him, and they meet with their forepaws raised, swiping. After the brief flash of violence, a series of low growls drift out onto the African savannah.

Jelwana has a bleeding nose. Ufudu goes back to the lioness who gets up and jogs away from him with her tail moving; he jogs after her. This flirtation, with Ufudu following like a puppy, takes place for most of the day. It's driving Ufudu mad and he imposes his dominance over his brothers with a few short sharp scraps. He lies down a few metres from her, still, except for his head, which lifts with every rustle she makes. And his eyes move between her, his brothers, and the other lioness under a sickle bush.

Finally, she stands up and stretches, arching her back and yawning, then runs in front of him with her backside near his face. Flicking her tail up, she runs again in front of him, takes a few steps, lifts her tail, and crouches low. He moves forward and over her; she stays prone and does not discourage him. He mounts her over her back, and bites the back of her neck. She growls, and he whines a loud cat whine that betrays him as he finishes his attempt to procreate. He dismounts; the pain of his barbed penis removal causes her to roll and swipe him with a paw. He stands tall above her, and she lies on her back; rolling and writhing, he takes a step to the left and collapses.

For three days, they copulate. For the first two days he mates with her every fifteen minutes. Ufudu slows down on the third day; he is exhausted. He relinquishes her, and Jelwana mates with her. Insele is mating with the other lioness. He tires after days. Ufudu has recovered enough to mate with her too.

After their rotating mating session, the lionesses return to the pride and the males wander towards their western boundary marking, roaring and spraying. They cross the Crocodile River and squeeze under a drainage line, striding through Marloth Park at night. They roar an earth-shattering roar that shakes windows and causes some residents to wake and murmur with fear in the comfort of their homes. Drinking out of a pool, they enter the Lionspruit reserve, marking and spraying, through their old haunts. They visit the vulture restaurant and nosh on a giraffe carcass. They roar and patrol, but there are no lionesses here.

They laze at the vulture restaurant for the day. Cars come and go to the news that the Lionspruit coalition has returned. As night falls, they find a warthog burrow under the fence, slide under, and stroll through Marloth Park. A person walks towards them in the night with a torch. The male lions move off and lie under the angular branches of a sandpaper raisin bush, with their heads up like the sphinx's. The person walks past without knowing that three adult male lions are staring at him in the darkness.

They pad toward the Crocodile River, walking past the opening that sustained them as youngsters. An ostrich is sleeping with its wing over its head. They kill it and eat it, but it is not enough food for three adult lions, so they head under the fence, over the Crocodile River under the cover of darkness.

Back in the Kruger, they roar their dominion and walk towards the east, spraying and marking as they move. In the morning light, they see vultures descending, and they follow, finding the Vurhami pride on a buffalo kill. They rush in with grunts and open mouths and the lionesses scatter off the meal. After they have eaten some, they allow the females to join on the opposite side of the carcass. After the feast, the lion pride lies with swollen bellies near the carcass. The Lionspruit males sleep it off. When they are feeling less bloated, they harass the young sub-adult male lion, charging at him, roaring, and chasing him when they feel like it. Not always – sometimes they stare at him. Sometimes they ignore him. They keep him on his toes, and the lionesses, sensing the change, are less tolerant of the young male.

The lead lioness with the collar starts to come closer, rubbing her head against them and showing keen interest. The males assess their condition and follow them as the lionesses lead them from the pride. They stroll towards the Gezantombi view site onto the open plains, overlooking the dam. An African fish eagle calls, throwing its head back.

The lead lioness is thirteen years old. The two younger lionesses are from the same litter and approaching six years of age. They have synchronised their oestrus, the younger lionesses compelled to come into heat by losing their cubs. The Lionspruit coalition does not fight, as each has a female to mate with, though the collared lioness gives Ufudu a scar on his cheek on one occasion when he pulls out his barbed penis. The mounting and mating take place around Gezantombi for three days, causing a host of pictures to be posted online, and debated on online chats. Facebook bloggers publish stories and make assumptions about the litter and the internet ignites with armchair lion enthusiasts.

It is nearing the end of winter and a puddle of water remains in the dam – one of the only puddles. Animals are drawn there to quench their thirst. The lionesses interrupt the honeymoon. A warthog strolls onto the animal spoor-peppered bank of the dam. The lions stalk from all corners. The speed at which a lion can go from mating or slumber to an opportunistic hunt is like flipping a switch. The warthog is evaluating the air, stopping and staring. It sees Ufudu watching from above, spins, and runs to safety with its tail up like a flag. The lionesses come back to their males and continue mating.

A striking bird named the orange-breasted bush shrike calls its call. Some call it the air hostess bird because if you use your imagination, it sounds like 'Coffee, tea or me?' which is apt for what is happening below the tree. A troop of baboons start barking at the cats, who ignore them, having other things on their minds. After a few minutes of barking, the baboons move off, realising their barks are about as effective as a Marloth activist group.

CHAPTER 36

After days of mating, with intermittent rests and partner exchanges, and micro rests, the lions observe vultures descending to the south and hunger spurs them to head over. A giraffe has been brought down, and the entire pride feasts on the large meal. Its stomach contents and fluids stain the ground around the carcass. The lions eat and laze for five days. The males recover from their vigorous mating assignments and every night they roar their ownership towards the corners of their territory.

Energy returns and the pull of the horizon. Walking north along the H4-2 past Gezantombi up a crest in the road where they once pulled down two zebras, they sense other males to the north have marked here. They roar but do not head north, announcing this is the accepted boundary and in the distance, they hear a response. The Lionspruit coalition gleans it is three male lions responding, older animals. They roar again in unison, and head east, marking along the boundaries of their territory, roaring, announcing 'This is ours, this is ours, this is ours...'

They go to the end of the Vurhami pride territory marking along the border and enter the Shishangeni pride territory. Two lionesses find them lazing in the heat of the day. The lions do their duty for four days, and when Ufudu tires, Jelwana takes over, spreading their genes.

The three male lions follow the lionesses to the pride and attach to the Shishangeni pride for a few weeks, eating meals provided by the lioness's hard work. Then the Lionspruit males walk up the Lebombo mountain past Lebombo iron-wood trees and rhyolite rocks. A giant gunmetal grey snake, the black mamba, slithers away from them. Insele rushes at it, but it disappears swiftly behind stones.

Coming to a large fence, they stare into Mozambique. The structure is enough of a bottleneck for them to mark along the road that follows it, satisfied this can be their eastern boundary. They roar into Mozambique but hear no response. The lionesses are in the grassland plains down below, and they return to them. They are on a zebra kill, and the males dominate the kill and then slumber.

Ufudu stands up one winter morning, stretches and yawns. Without waiting for his brothers, he heads west to the Hippo Pools pride where he entrenches himself. Insele and Jelwana attach to the Vurhami pride. They contact each other with roars when they feel compelled to. They do territorial patrols covering larger areas, some by themselves and sometimes together.

Ufudu finds the one sub-adult from the Vurhami in the Hippo Pool territory and chases after him. The young male bolts from Ufudu. His hips are showing, and the youngster needs to find a meal soon. His loneliness after his expulsion from the pride is compounded as he has no brothers with him. The young lion leaves the Hippo Pools territory and heads west.

The rulers eat, sleep, patrol and fight. One hundred and ten days after their mating marathons there are no results as the lionesses did not get pregnant – no births, not even one. When the lionesses show oestrus again the lions revolve around the prides and mate again.

This time they are successful and sixteen weeks later, little furballs of approximately 1.5 kilograms start appearing in den sites throughout the territory. Some of the cubs' eyes open three days after birth in the dense den sites and a few days later, all the eyes are open. They start walking eleven days after birth and exploring their surroundings.

The litters sired by the Lionspruit coalition grow. Creches form in the prides that these males rule, filled with playful balls of energy that take in the wide world of the African bush. The lionesses look after them with gentle instinctive care, in such contrast to their savagery during a kill – they can tear into a huge animal with teeth, claws and courage, but lovingly nurture a tiny cub, including licking their cub's anal area to stimulate the nerves and facilitate bowel movements. They are fiercely protective moms.

The males are in their prime and provide strong rulership, and stability for the lionesses. The males are licked, nuzzled, groomed and included in the pride. Young lions pass through but never try to stay. On the rare occasions that the Lionspruit coalition picks up a fresh scent, they chase until resolution is achieved – either from posturing on occasion, or claw and fang on others. Once, they kill two young males slumbering in the day under a magic guarri bush. Lions in their prime can hear by the number of different roars that there is no vacuum in these pride lands... yet.

The cubs have Shishangeni and Gomodwane coalitions blood from their mothers, and the Lionspruit coalition blood from their fathers. Robust, diverse and genetically viable blood. The Lionspruit coalition is indifferent to the young lions they fathered when they joined the pride. They smell them and are satisfied they are kin. On rare occasions, Jelwana, Ufudu and Insele swish the dark ends of their tails to titillate a youngster.

But somewhere in the bush, others are looking to the horizon and the end of the Lionspruit coalition. No matter how mighty, the outcome is written in the short harsh world of the lion. But this part of the world still has wild lions living and thriving. The cycle continues for now, and you can still hear the call of ownership echoing out over the African plains. A sound that comes from deep inside the belly of a lion. An incredibly powerful sound.

One you should experience at least once in your life.

BIBLIOGRAPHY

Branch, W.R (2008). *Tortoises, terrapins & turtles of Africa.* Cape Town: Struik Publishers.

Burgess, G., Ferreira, S., Talukdar, B., Knight, M., Baruch-Mordo, S., & Ellis, S. (2022). African and Asian Rhinoceroses: Status, Conservation and Trade: Report from the IUCN Species Survival Commission (IUCN SSC) African and Asian Rhino Specialist Groups and TRAFFIC (CITES CoP19 Doc 75).

Bygott, J. D., Bertram, B. C., & Hanby, J. P. (1979). Male lions in large coalitions gain reproductive advantages. *Nature, 282*(5741), 839-841.

Chardonnet, P., Soto, B., Fritz, H., Crosmary, W., Drouet-Hoguet, N., Mesochina, P., ... & Lamarque, F. (2010). Managing the conflicts between people and lion. *Review and insights from the literature and field experience.*

Drea, C. M., Coscia, E. M., & Glickman, S. E. (2018). *Hyenas.*

Funston, P. J., Mills, M. G., Richardson, P. R., & van Jaarsveld, A. S. (2003). Reduced dispersal and opportunistic territory acquisition in male lions (Panthera leo). *Journal of Zoology, 259*(2), 131-142.

Furstenburg, D. (2012). Focus on the Lion (Panthera leo). *Geo Wild Consult*, 1-17.

Green, J., Jakins, C., Waal, L. D., & D'Cruze, N. (2021). Ending commercial lion farming in South Africa: A gap analysis approach. *Animals, 11*(6), 1717.

Grinnell, J., & McComb, K. (2001). Roaring and social communication in African lions: The limitations imposed by listeners. *Animal Behaviour, 62*(1), 93-98.

Heinsohn, R. (1997). Group territoriality in two populations of African lions. *Animal behaviour, 53*(6), 1143-1147.

Houston, D. C., & Cooper, J. E. (1975). The digestive tract of the whiteback griffon vulture and its role in disease transmission among wild ungulates. *Journal of wildlife diseases*, *11*(3), 306-313.

Hutson, J. M., Burke, C. C., & Haynes, G. (2013). Osteophagia and bone modifications by giraffe and other large ungulates. *Journal of Archaeological Science*, *40*(12), 4139-4149.

Klemuk, S. A., Riede, T., Walsh, E. J., & Titze, I. R. (2011). Adapted to roar: Functional morphology of tiger and lion vocal folds. *PloS one*, *6*(11), e27029.

Lesku, J. A., Meyer, L. C., Fuller, A., Maloney, S. K., Dell'Omo, G., Vyssotski, A. L., & Rattenborg, N. C. (2011). Ostriches sleep like platypuses. *PloS one*, *6*(8), e23203.

Maruping-Mzileni, N. T., Ferreira, S., Young, K., & Funston, P. J. (2020). Ecological drivers of female lion (Panthera leo) reproduction in the Kruger National Park. *Ecology and Evolution*, *10*(15), 7995-8006.

McComb, K., Packer, C., & Pusey, A. (1994). Roaring and numerical assessment in contests between groups of female lions, Panthera leo. *Animal Behaviour*, *47*(2), 379-387.

Mosser, A., & Packer, C. (2009). Group territoriality and the benefits of sociality in the African lion, Panthera leo. *Animal Behaviour*, *78*(2), 359-370.

Nams, V. O., Parker, D. M., Weise, F. J., Patterson, B. D., Buij, R., Radloff, F. G., ... & Beukes, M. (2023). Spatial patterns of large African cats: A large-scale study on density, home range size, and home range overlap of lions Panthera leo and leopards Panthera pardus. *Mammal Review*, *53*(2), 49-64.

O'Connell-Rodwell, C. E., Wood, J. D., Kinzley, C., Rodwell, T. C., Poole, J. H., & Puria, S. (2007). Wild African elephants (Loxodonta africana) discriminate between familiar and unfamiliar conspecific seismic alarm calls. *The Journal of the Acoustical Society of America*, *122*(2), 823-830.

Oliver, C. M. (2006). *The role of the ram in the impala (Aepyceros melampus) mating system* [Doctoral dissertation, University of Pretoria].

BIBLIOGRAPHY

Packer, C. (2023). *The lion: Behavior, ecology, and conservation of an iconic species*. Princeton University Press.

Packer, C., & Pusey, A. E. (1983). Male takeovers and female reproductive parameters: A simulation of oestrous synchrony in lions (Panthera leo). *Animal Behaviour, 31*(2), 334-340.

Packer, C., & Pusey, A. E. (1982). Cooperation and competition within coalitions of male lions: Kin selection or game theory?. *Nature, 296*(5859), 740-742.

Pardo, M., Fristrup, K., Lolchuragi, D., Poole, J., Granli, P., Moss, C., Douglas-Hamilton, I., & Wittemyer, G. (2024). African elephants address one another with individually specific name-like calls. *Nature Ecology & Evolution, 8*.

Poole, J. H., & Moss, C. J. (1981). Musth in the African elephant, Loxodonta Africana. *Nature, 292*(5826), 830-831.

Scheel, D., & Packer, C. (1991). Group hunting behaviour of lions: A search for cooperation. *Animal behaviour, 41*(4), 697-709.

Smuts, G. L., Hanks, J., & Whyte, I. J. (1978). Reproduction and social organization of lions from the Kruger National Park. *Carnivore, 1*(JAN), 17-28.

Tajuddeen, N., Swart, T., Hoppe, H. C., & van Heerden, F. R. (2022). Antiplasmodial activity of vachellia xanthophloea (benth). PJH Hurter (African fever tree) and its constituents. *Pharmaceuticals, 15*(4), 470.

West, P. M., & Packer, C. (2002). Sexual selection, temperature, and the lion's mane. *Science, 297*(5585), 1339–1343.

Wijers, M., Trethowan, P., Du Preez, B., Chamaillé-Jammes, S., Loveridge, A. J., Macdonald, D. W., & Markham, A. (2021). The influence of spatial features and atmospheric conditions on African lion vocal behaviour. *Animal Behaviour, 174*, 63-76.

ACKNOWLEDGMENTS

I would be remiss to not thank the guests of Honey Badger Safaris I have hosted through the years, for if it were not for them, I would not have spent as much time in the bush as I have. Thanks are also due to SANParks as the custodians of the Kruger National Park.

Tracy Buenk, my editor, who saved me from blushing. My family, particularly my parents who instilled a love for wilderness from a young age.

Thanks to David Henderson, Gregg Davies and Malcolm Coombes for the efforts on this book, I appreciate it.

The researchers, guides and conservationists who study the lion and other animals, providing knowledge and insight that I have regurgitated to many guests over the years, often pretending it came to me in a dream.

And to you the reader. Thank you. Maybe I can take you around the Kruger one of these days on safari? Your visit to these places keeps them feasible.

ABOUT THE AUTHOR

Jonathan Couzens was born in Zululand, South Africa. At the age of sixteen, his parents opened a lodge in Phalaborwa, near the Kruger National Park, which is when his interest in wildlife took hold.

He was a director of a corporate business in Mozambique for a time but co-founded Honey Badger Safaris in 2013 and since then has been observing and discussing the animals he writes about in this book.

His wildlife photography and videos can be seen on Instagram at @jonathancouzens and @honeybadgersafaris.

This is his debut novel.

You can join him on safari at www.honeybadgersafaris.co.za

HONEY BADGER
SAFARIS

Made in the USA
Las Vegas, NV
17 September 2024

95390731R00121